After All is Said and Done....
More is Said Than Done

Carla Reed

PublishAmerica
Baltimore

© 2011 by Carla Reed.
All rights reserved. No part of this book may be reproduced, stored in a retrieval system or transmitted in any form or by any means without the prior written permission of the publishers, except by a reviewer who may quote brief passages in a review to be printed in a newspaper, magazine or journal.

First printing

All characters in this book are fictitious, and any resemblance to real persons, living or dead, is coincidental.

PublishAmerica has allowed this work to remain exactly as the author intended, verbatim, without editorial input.

Softcover 9781462648115
PUBLISHED BY PUBLISHAMERICA, LLLP
www.publishamerica.com
Baltimore

Printed in the United States of America

"A woman is like a tea bag. You never know how strong she is until she's in hot water."

—Eleanor Roosevelt

To my family and friends.

By the goodness of our Precious Lord and Savior, I am forgiven for my human shortcomings. And by his Grace I have been blessed beyond measure with family and friends that I love so dearly, and I will never take that for granted.

The words of this book were written by God's inspiration. I'm not a writer, so the words must be His. That's the only explanation I can come up with for the reason I was able to put these words on paper. I hope that after reading this book you will know that God can do anything in your life – just open your heart and let him in.

A special Thanks to my daughters, Kyla and Denise, for your encouragement to proceed with having my book published

If it hadn't been for your gentle pushing, the manuscript would still be collecting dust.

—Carla Reed

After All is Said and Done....
More is Said Than Done

PART 1

After All is Said and Done....More is Said Than Done

Chapter 1

What a day. Everything had been moved to the new house, but nothing was put up. Boxes stacked everywhere, beds unassembled, and furniture sitting wherever the movers could find a spot.

Thirty-three year old Candice Caps, or Candy as her friends called her, had packed up and left Texas with her two kids in tow. She had all she could stand of her alcoholic husband and his crazy family. She left a good job as an office manager for a clothing supplier behind, but she decided enough was enough, and she headed home to Oklahoma.

The little Town of Hereford, Oklahoma was where she was raised, and her parents still lived. She was the youngest of six, and all five of her siblings still lived in Oklahoma. They all lived within an hour of Hereford. Seth and Maggie lived in Tulsa, Natalee just outside of Hereford, and James and Annie lived by Lake Eufaula. Seth, Maggie, and Candy's parents had weekend homes at the lake.

Candice knew if she moved back to her hometown she would have her family to support her, and help with the kids. She was the first of her family to ever divorce. She had given the marriage a go for fourteen years, but her husband's abuse had become violent. She had always said that as long as she could hide Charlie's alcoholism and abuse from their children, she wouldn't leave him. She made a commitment to God to be married to him for the rest of her life, and she would do that. But the time had come, now that Cale, who was 4, and Abby who was 7, had witnessed one of their Dad's drunken fits.

Charlie Caps was a good guy when Candy married him, or at least he pretended to be. A week into their marriage Candy knew she had made a mistake. Candy hurried home from work to make dinner. She was young, only 19 years old, but she wanted to be a good wife to Charlie. Dinner was ready, the table was set, but no Charlie. Candy was getting worried. She called Charlie's job, but they said he had left work hours ago. She called Charlie's parents, but they hadn't seen him. By the time Charlie showed up at midnight, Candy was frantic.

"Where have you been, I've been worried sick about you!"

Charlie's speech was so slurred that Candy could barely understand him.

"I just stopped off for a beer with the guys."

"Oh my gosh! You're drunk!"

Charlie just looked at her and grinned. Candy just couldn't believe Charlie had done this. She started to cry.

"Why would you do this Charlie?"

Charlie just walked away. He went to their bedroom and laid on the bed. By the time Candy walked into the bedroom he was already snoring.

The next morning Candy told Charlie that she thought she had made a mistake by marrying him. Charlie apologized and promised never to do it again.

Charlie would sometimes just disappear for a few days. When he'd return he would beg Candy to forgive him. He would promise to be good to her, and she believed him. Sometimes he was good to her. They had a couple of vacations that were fun, but his good behavior never lasted very long. Charlie just couldn't stay sober.

Candy never knew what Charlie was going to be like when he got home - if he came home. He stopped at a bar almost every night on his way home from work "just to have a beer with his friends", but it always turned into a drunken stupor that Candy had to protect her kids from.

After All is Said and Done....More is Said Than Done

Candy always made excuses to friends and family for Charlie. She was good at pretending that all was well in the Caps home.

One night Charlie came in drunk but it wasn't real late like usual. *Guess they ran out of beer at the bar or something*, Candy thought. Candy cautiously went about cooking dinner and taking care of the kid's needs. Charlie kept saying off color things in front of the kids about the news report on TV. Candy said "Charlie, don't talk like that in front of Abby and Cale." Charlie just gave Candy an angry look, kicked back in his recliner and closed his eyes. Abby was sitting at the coffee table coloring. She moved a vase sitting on the coffee table, and it made a little noise. Charlie quickly raised up in his recliner and yelled some obscenities. Abby looked startled. Candy was furious. Candy calmly and caringly said to Abby, "Why don't you go on to bed now. You can leave your coloring book there and finish it tomorrow sweetheart." Abby, still confused about her Daddy's actions, did as she was told.

After the kids were sleeping soundly, Candy woke Charlie up to have another horrible fight with him. Candy knew that if she just left him alone, that tomorrow he would apologize, get her and the kids gifts, take them some place. It happened all the time. But she couldn't let it go. He had hurt her child. Candy told him that she was leaving him. Charlie looked at Candy like he hated her. Then he hissed, "You'll never find anyone else to put up with you. You're the reason I drink. I'm not hurting anyone by hanging out with my friends. You're just jealous because you don't have any friends. You can't make it without me Candy. You need me."

Candy was sitting in a chair. She was telling Charlie what a horrible example he was to their children, and she was not going to let them be subjected to it anymore. Charlie walked over to where Candy was sitting and picked her up - chair and all. Candy was fighting but Charlie was a big guy. Candy was only five feet two inches tall and weighed 100 pounds. Charlie carried her in the chair to the door and literally threw her, and the chair, out the back door. Candy jumped up, but before she could get to the door Charlie had it locked. Candy was frantic. She had to get in there. Her kids were in there. She banged on the door. Begged him to open it. Crying, screaming, begging. Charlie finally walked out the door, got in his truck and left. Candy ran into the house and locked the doors. She started packing up all of her, and the kid's, things.

The next morning Charlie called. "Candy I'm going away for a few days. We just need some time apart." Candy said, "You don't have to Charlie, because me and the kids are moving to Oklahoma. It's time for us to end this." Charlie actually agreed and told Candy that she could have everything. The only thing he wanted was his personal things, clothes and such. Candy hired movers, quit her job, and left the next day. It was time to go. God would understand.

Charlie called a couple of times after Candy left, but he had better things to do than to think about her and the kids. He basically disappeared from their lives, and that was okay with Candy. Even though she knew it hurt the kids in the beginning, it was better for Charlie to just leave them alone then to be in and out of their lives. She knew that Charlie could never be a good father to her kids. He would only continue to disappoint them. Charlie knew it too.

Chapter 2

Standing with her hands on her hips, her long sandy colored hair in a braid with loose strands of hair falling around her face, and little sweat beads on her freckled face, Candy was deciding what to do first when the doorbell rang. She figured it was her Mom, or one of her sisters coming to offer help, but she couldn't figure out why they wouldn't just come on in. Surprised and happy to see longtime friend Larry Baker at her door, she told him to excuse all the clutter, and moved some things so he could sit in a kitchen chair. Candy had known Larry most of her life. She babysat his twin girls when she was a teen. Sometimes when Larry would come home, after Candy had been watching the girls, she would talk to him for hours about her teenage problems. He was about fifty years old now. He was short, a little overweight and losing some of that thick black hair, but that happy smile of his was still there.

Candy thought Larry had just come by to welcome her back, but he was on a mission. Larry was now the Town Mayor. Hereford's population had really grown. There were 2,457 people according to the latest census. Of course being Mayor was not Larry's real job. He was a real estate agent, and was rarely in Town. He did most of his business in the neighboring cities.

Larry had a problem that he just knew Candy could help him with. They were having trouble finding someone to replace the City Clerk. She had recently gotten married, and moved to Oklahoma City. They had a woman who had been the City Clerk 15 years ago filling in. She had long been retired, and everything had changed, so she really wasn't able to do much except answer the phone and put people off.

"Candy will you please consider taking this job. With your experience in office management, I know you would be great. We really need someone who is smart and knows the basics". Larry had his most persuasive smile plastered on his face. Gosh she was a sucker for compliments, and he knew it.

"I really don't know anything about Municipal Government, but I guess I could try it. If it doesn't work out we'll both know it. I really do need a job."

An answer to prayer! Candy had no idea what she would do about supporting her kids, but she knew she would do it with God guiding her, and here on her first day in town was the answer.

Larry told her that he would call a special meeting of the city council to discuss hiring her, and he would give her a call in a couple of days. Then they said their goodbyes.

Well, if she was going to work in a couple of days she had better get busy putting this stuff away.

After Cale and Abby had their baths, Candy spent some time talking to them about their new life in Oklahoma. Cale looked just like his mother. A little guy with blond hair, blue eyes and freckles. Just precious to look at. Abby had dark brown hair like her father. That was the only thing about her that was like him. She was a beautiful little girl. She was going to be taller than her mother, and pretty, not cute like Candy.

Now that the kids were tucked in and sleeping angels, it was time to get to work. Candy would get most of their things put away tonight, and her sister Natalee would be over tomorrow to help her finish up. Thank goodness for family, Candy thought.

Before she realized it, it was 3:30 A.M. Candy was still hard at it, putting things away, when she decided she really should call it quits for the night. She had her bedroom pretty much done, and that soft bed sure looked enticing. She was so tired that she laid down on the bed, not even taking time to take a shower, or put on pajamas. She figured she'd have so many things swirling in her mind about the new job, new home, and everything in between, that she wouldn't sleep a wink. But she was totally unconscious until Cale woke her up wanting to get into bed with her at 8:00 A.M.

Two days later Candy and the kids were at her parents' house when Larry saw her car there. He had just left the city council meeting.

"Candy, the city council voted unanimously to hire you. They want to give you full benefits right away which includes insurance and retirement, vacation and sick leave. They want you to start tomorrow."

Candy felt like she would get the job, but still just hearing out loud what God was doing in her life made her want to shout praises.

"What time do you want me there Larry. I need to make arrangements for the kids."

Candy's Mom said she'd keep them during the day while Candy worked.

"Well, I guess that takes care of that" Candy replied. It would be so perfect.

Larry told her to be at city hall at 8:00 A.M. "We also hired another woman named Rita Matthews. One of the other council members actually talked to her before I got a chance to talk to you, so she was offered the position of Office Manager. Your position will be the City Clerk. But don't worry about it, you'll like her okay. She's a little different, but you can get along with anyone. She won't give you any trouble, I promise. If she does, let me know and I'll take care of it."

That had Candy a little worried, but not too much. She got along well with most everyone.

Chapter 3

Candy started her new job the next day. City hall was a red brick building built in 1918 on the corner of Main Street. It was the typical red brick building on every corner, in every town across America. The inside had been recently remodeled by volunteers. Hereford took a lot of pride in the old building. It was the oldest building still standing in the town. As you walked in the front door, there was an area for customers to wait their turn. Usually there was only one customer at a time, but on the first of the month there would sometimes be two or three people just hanging around in the front lobby so they could visit.

The entryway still had the original tiles on the floor. They were in a mosaic style that was common for the era that the building was built in.

There was a counter that divided the lobby from the workers desks. There were two desks. One for Candy, and one for Rita.

Behind the desks were dividers. On the other side of the dividers was a long table that was used by the City Council to conduct their monthly meetings. It was also used for Municipal Court which was held the first Thursday of each month at 10:00 A.M.

Beyond the meeting area, were four offices, a supply closet, and in the corner was the bathroom.

Only one of the offices was used. The City Council used it to go into closed executive session if they had something secret to talk about. According to state law there are specific guidelines on what you can go into executive session for. It didn't take Candy long to figure out that the city council didn't follow state statutes on a lot of things, and executive session

After All is Said and Done....More is Said Than Done

was one of them. They thought they could say they were going into executive session without any explanation as to why, and discuss everything from buying a new tractor to the cost of corn over at the market.

Rita was a very tall, very slender woman, with black spiky hair and tons of makeup. She was pretty obnoxious, but Candy could handle her. Candy learned how to deal with her by ignoring her most of the time.

There were five council members including Larry. They all had regular jobs besides serving on the City Council. Mayor was really just a glorified title. Although the title meant little to nothing, Larry led people to believe that being Mayor was quite prestigious. Hereford was a town form of Government, which basically meant that no council member had any more authority than the other. The only thing different for the Mayor was that he conducted the council meetings and signed official documents - with the other council member's approval.

Almost every day a couple of the council members would come by city hall on their way to work. They just dropped in to visit, and to see if the citizens were complaining about anything. They didn't know much about the actual work that went on at City Hall. When Candy or Rita would have them sign something, most of the time they didn't even know what they were signing. The only time they were all together was council meeting night. That was usually a circus. The council members would pretend to know the laws of municipal government. Rita would try to tell them what to do. The council would get mad at Rita. Rita would get mad at the council. They'd sometimes yell at each other, and Candy would try to make peace. Rita was very opinionated, to say the least, and she thought she was expert on most all subjects. That caused some very heated council meetings. It was really quite funny sometimes.

It didn't take Candy long to get settled into her new job. The people of Hereford seemed to be glad that she had decided to come back home.

Learning all the ins and outs of municipal government took time and effort. Candy was a little overwhelmed when she found out that even though Hereford was a small town, they still had to abide by the same laws as Oklahoma City or Tulsa. She figured out right away that it was not going to be a small task to learn all she needed to know to be good at her job. Almost every night when Candy said her prayers she said "Lord, if this is where I'm supposed to be, show me the way. Open my mind to learn all that I need to learn, and help me to be good at my job. Lord, I will do all that you ask of me. I am so thankful for this job, and I give you all the glory."

She started reading Oklahoma State Statute books. She practically memorized Title 11 which was everything relating to municipal town form of government. She read every piece of legislative updates that came through the office. She went to training conferences. God was giving her all the opportunities she needed to learn, and she was accepting them.

Delores Black was a retired nurse, and the town head volunteer and social chairman. Delores was a short heavyset woman with bad knees. She had salt and pepper hair, and she would not be caught out in public without her makeup on and her hair done. She was a leader for any, and every, organization in town. She made sure that dinners were arranged for families if there was a death, she organized the Christmas parade, she started the "Friends of the Library" group, she was head of fund raisers, and everyone loved her.

When Delores heard that Candy had moved back and was working at City Hall, she couldn't wait to welcome her home.

After All is Said and Done....More is Said Than Done

"Candy, it is so good to see you again. I just heard that you moved back and I wanted to tell you how happy we are that your here. I've heard some nice things about you, and it wasn't all from your Mother either." She had a broad smile as she spoke.

"Ohhhhh. Thank you Delores. I'm glad to be back. The longer I was gone, the more I wanted to come home."

Almost everyone who came into city hall greeted Candy in the same way. They were happy she was there, and she sure was happy she was too.

Rita seemed a little miffed that everyone liked Candy so much. She had a real habit of trying to belittle Candy in front of people. Every time Candy was on the phone with someone about city business, Rita butted in and said things like, "*Do you need me to help you with that.....*"

Rita was one of the most annoying people Candy had ever met. She didn't just annoy Candy though. She shared her personality with everyone she came in contact with.

The town was having some work done on the sidewalk in front of city hall to meet the ADA requirements (Americans with Disabilities Act). The man who was doing the work was a longtime resident. An older gentleman who had been doing cement work his entire adult life. Gary was a very nice, quiet man. Candy just thought the world of him. He would step into city hall every once in a while to take a break and visit with Candy.

One morning Candy saw Rita outside talking to Gary. She could see Rita waving her arms and pointing to the sidewalk. She put her hands on her hips, then pointed, then waved her arms, then pointed...... Candy noticed that Gary seemed to be ignoring her. He continued to smooth the cement as Rita was giving him instructions.

Later that day, Gary came in for a break while Rita was gone to lunch. He said, "You know, that poor crazy thing, she came out there and was telling me how to do that sidewalk. Candy, I've been doing mud work for forty years. I finally told her to go on back inside and leave me alone. She's a real peace of work. Bless her heart, maybe she don't even know she's crazy. I don't know how you can stand to work with her."

Candy had to laugh. "I ignore her a lot. I practice selective hearing."

"Boy, you'd have to. I couldn't do it. I'm going to start calling her Maytag."

"Maytag?"

"Yea, she's just an agitator."

Then they both laughed.

One day Candy was working on a letter to the Department of Environmental Quality. Rita asked "What are you doing Hun?"Rita thought she had to know what Candy was doing at all times.

Candy immediately got angry. She knew if she said anything, it would be too much. She got up and walked away from her desk. She decided it was break time – right now!

Rita called out "Hun are you okay".

Candy kept walking. That's how she had to deal with Rita. Otherwise it would get ugly. Under Candy's breath she repeated over and over, "Walk away, ignore her, don't say it, don't say it….."

***

Rita not only thought she needed to tell Candy how to do her job. She also got a little personal sometimes. "Hun, what kind of makeup do you wear?"

Candy didn't want to answer because she knew whatever she said wouldn't be the end of the conversation. After a little hesitation, Candy said, "Whatever is on sale."

"You really should be using something with a lot of water in it. The water adds moisture to your skin. The older you get, the more water you need. You don't want to wait too long to get into a good cleansing program either."

In a frustrated tone, Candy said, "Okay, I'll think about that." She was thinking, *where in the world did that come from.*

***

Every day around 2 o'clock Rita would say, "I just have to take a short break. I'm going to just lay on the couch for a few minutes."

There was an old couch sitting along the back wall of city hall. Rita got it somewhere and brought it to city hall so she'd have somewhere to sit and "take a break" as she'd say. Rita would lay down on that old couch, and before her head hit the armrest she'd be asleep. And then the snoring would start! Candy had put up with that as long as she could.

Candy stomped over to the couch and said, " Good Grief Rita!!! If you have to sleep everyday maybe you should stay home! Your snoring is really embarrassing when a customer comes in."

Candy stormed back to her desk. Rita got up off the couch and went back to her desk. From then on when she needed her afternoon nap, she went into the back office and sat in a chair.

At the end of each day, Candy and Rita balanced the cash drawer and did a report for the water department. It was Rita's turn to balance the cash drawer while Candy worked on the report. Candy was doing her report when she heard a crash. She turned quickly to see that Rita had fallen out of her chair and knocked the cash drawer on the floor. Coins went every which direction. Candy hurried over to help Rita off the floor.

"Rita ! Are you okay?"

"I'm okay, I just fell asleep."

Candy started picking up all the money as Rita got back into her chair. Even though Candy was aggravated at Rita, she knew something was wrong. Candy and Rita talked about her having to sleep every day, and now this.

"I just don't know what's wrong with me. I fell asleep driving the other day."

"Rita, maybe you should see a doctor. Do you sleep well at night?"

"No, I'm up half the night. Sometimes I get on my bicycle and ride out to the truck stop at night. I just sit out there in a booth and read. Sometimes I talk to the truckers that come in there."

"Oh my gosh! You shouldn't be out on your bike that time of night. I know Hereford's a pretty calm place but things happen."

"I'm not scared. I've met some pretty nice people while I was out there. One guy said he's gonna call me and take me to dinner the next time he comes through."

"Oh, good grief. One of these days you're gonna go off with someone and we're never gonna see you again. "

Rita told Candy that she had been thinking about seeing a doctor about this falling asleep thing.

A couple of weeks later she did see a Dr. and sure enough she had a problem with the production of melatonin in her brain. Once she got treatment for her problem she started sleeping at night, and the afternoon naps stopped. She quit hanging around the truck stop late at night. That is on week nights anyway. Now the weekends- that was a different story.

Chapter 4

The kids just loved spending time with Candy's Mom and Dad. They called them Mama and Papa. Cale and his Papa had formed quite a bond. Little as Cale was, he would spend hours watching westerns and baseball with Papa. It was such a special time for them. Once school started. Candy would take the kids to school then head off to work. Mama would pick them up from school and keep them until Candy got off work. Weekends were spent at Lake Eufaula. Mama and Papa had a cabin right next door to Candy's sister, Annie. Everyone congregated at the lake on the weekends. Life was pretty good for Candy, Cale and Abby.

***

There was a police officer named Alvin Patterson working for the Town of Hereford that usually worked nights, but sometimes he would come into city hall during the day to finish up a report, or to just see if anything was going on in the booming metropolis of Hereford. Everyone called him Pat.

He came in to city hall one afternoon after Candy had been working there for a couple of weeks. As Candy reached to shake his hand she said, "Hi, you must be Pat. I've heard so much about you, and all of it was good. I'm Candy, the new City Clerk." He shook her hand and shyly said, "Very nice to meet you Candy." Pat was a little surprised by Candy's friendly approach. He was a reserved kind of guy. He thought, this girl is a breath of fresh air in this place.

After Pat left the office, Rita looked over her reading glasses at Candy. She had a look on her face like something smelled bad.

"I don't like that guy. He reminds me so much of my ex-husband."

"Really, in what way."

"Oh, he looks kind of like him, and just his mannerisms."

Candy was thinking, *"yea, and I bet he don't like you either."*

Pat's wife had died in a tragic car crash three years earlier, and Candy's previous marriage had ultimately ended in a tragedy of sorts, so they seemed to connect. Candy was working late one night when Pat came into work. They started talking. Pat talked about his wife. Candy talked about her ex-husband, and her life in Texas. Pat felt sorry for Candy for all she had been through.

"Candy I really admire you for being able to suck it up and move on with your life. "

"Oh, thanks Pat, but I really didn't do it for me. It was all for my kids. There's nothing more important to me than them. If you were a parent you'd understand. Well, I don't guess that's necessarily true, since my kid's dad didn't think they were very important. You know he actually told me one time that he guessed I just loved them more than he did."

Pat looked angry and shook his head. He couldn't believe anyone could say that about their own kids.

"Wow, that's a terrible thing to say. I can't imagine. He's such a jerk."

"Yea, he is, but that's behind us now."

Pat was pretty shy, but for some reason it was just so easy for him to talk to Candy. He was very handsome, with dark curly hair and pale blue eyes. He was average height but he looked tall in his uniform. He was so kind to people, but he never socialized. That is until Candy came along. She brought the best out in him. They started dating and the whole town was abuzz, but they didn't care what people said. They really liked each other.

One day a friend of Candy's saw her getting out of her car and came over to talk to her.

"Candy, do you really think you should be dating so soon after your divorce? You know some people don't think it looks too good."

Candy paused a moment to compose her temper, then said, "I don't really care what people think. I like Pat, and I'm going to be with him, so if people don't like it, it's their problem, not mine!"

And that was that. The word got out pretty quickly that it was best not to mention Candy's personal life to her.

As Candy and Pat's relationship grew, so did Pat's relationship with her kids. They went to the zoo, had picnics, and Pat was even included in their weekends at the lake with Candy's family. It was inevitable that they would be together for the rest of their lives.

They had been dating for six months, when one night while watching TV, Pat said "Candy let's get married. "

The next day was Friday. They decided they would go to Fort Smith, Arkansas the next morning, since you could get your license and be married there on the same day. In Oklahoma you had to have blood tests, get a license, and wait a week for your blood test results.

The next morning Candy told the kids that she and Pat were getting married. She called Rita at the office and told her that she was taking a vacation day. She got the kids off to school. Dressed in some jeans and a cute gray long sleeved top with ruffles down the front. She braided her hair and put on a little make up, and as she looked in the mirror she thought, *"Charlie, you were wrong. Someone does love me."* Pat was the man that Candy had hoped Charlie could be, but never was. Pat loved her, and would take care of her, Abby, and Cale for the rest of their lives. Candy was so happy. So many things were going right in her life. Today was her wedding day.

Chapter 5

Being the City Clerk, Candy did a little of everything that needed to be done. One of her jobs was to serve as the Court Clerk. One day Larry called Candy and said " Hey Candy, I have a guy working for me who got a ticket for reckless driving in Hereford. He'll get his driver's license suspended if that ticket goes on his record. I can't have him working for me without a license. Is there anything you can do?"

Candy knew this was going to be a touchy situation but she had to do what was right. "That ticket has already been sent to the Department of Public Safety. The only way to get it off his record would be for me to send a notice to DPS saying that I made a mistake. The judge already found him guilty Larry."

Larry hesitated a second, "Well why don't you go ahead and do that for me - send a notice to DPS".

Candy was stunned. She said " Well, okay", but she knew she wasn't going to do it.

That night she told Pat about the conversation with Larry. Pat was furious. He could not believe that Larry would ask Candy to do something illegal. He said "Candy, do you know who would be in trouble if it got out that you did that? Not Larry, not the other council members, not me for writing the ticket, YOU! You cannot do that! I can't believe Larry would ask you to do that!"

Pat then went to his office, took off his badge and laid it on his desk. He called Larry and gave him an ear full. "Larry, you don't need to say anything, because I know that whatever comes out of your mouth will be a lie, so you just listen to what I have to say".

Larry was so surprised by the phone call that he didn't know whether to just hang up and pretend the line was disconnected, or to start lying. Instead, he just said, "What's wrong Pat?"

Pat was trying very hard to control his temper. "I cannot believe you would ask Candy to send false information to the State of Oklahoma. She thinks the world of you. You might have her fooled about what kind of person you are, but it's pretty clear to me. I won't work another day for the Town of Hereford as long as you have any part of it. My badge is on my desk." Then Pat hung up the phone.

***

Candy didn't send the notice to DPS. Larry knew he had messed up, but he would never have admitted it. Candy and Pat both knew that if the story ever got out, Larry would deny it. Candy was pretty shocked to know the real Larry. Still, he was her friend, and she'd just let it go.

It never got around town the real reason that Pat quit. Pat went to work for the County Sheriff, which was a better deal for him anyway. He was trained to work drug interdiction, and it gave him an opportunity to use his skills. When one door closes, God opens another one for you.

***

Candy began to notice that Larry made comments at the council meetings that weren't true. When he was confronted about making a decision without council approval, he'd deny it. He always seemed to look out for himself and let someone else take the fall. When he knew he was going to be confronted about something he had done, he would conveniently have to be out of town and couldn't be reached. Larry was always doing things that were borderline illegal.

Some of the city workers had begun to notice some things missing from the shop building. They stored street equipment, and just a little bit of everything in there. At the side of the building there was a 250 gallon diesel tank they would get diesel out of for the tractors. One day the tank was gone. A street worker named Brandon, told Candy that the tank was gone. He said, "I know where it is though."

Candy said, "What do you mean, you know where it is?"

Brandon hesitated a little, then said, "Well, I did some checking around, and someone who knows someone, said that Larry gave it to a guy that works for him. He said the guy needed it to fuel his farm equipment. I guess they came in the evening when everyone was gone, and loaded it on a trailer or something."

Candy knew it was illegal to give away city property, but she didn't want to cause any trouble for Larry. She said, "Brandon, does anyone else know about this?"

He said, "Yea, the other guys who work with me knows about it. We're pretty aggravated too. It sure made it convenient for us to fill our tractors with diesel. Now we'll have to drive the tractors over to the station to buy diesel. Guess it don't do any good to get mad though. Seems like Larry can do whatever he wants to do. I hit Larry up about it, and he said he didn't think we used it anymore."

Candy decided to just keep her mouth shut about the diesel tank. Once again she was protecting Larry.

Larry and a council member named Chester Davis took turns being Mayor. Every two years there was an election for city council members. After an election all the council members would decide who would be Mayor for the next two years. Larry and Chester had both been council members for more than fifteen years. They never drew an opponent so they were a shoe-in every election. Nobody in their right mind wanted to be on the city council. They got paid $5 a month to come to a meeting once a month and fight with each other.

Chester took an interest in the police department. He really liked Pat. In fact, they had become good friends. Chester didn't have much use for Larry after Pat resigned.

The council members rarely agreed on things, but they did actually agree on one project, and that was to build a park on a vacant lot that the town owned. Candy got a grant to buy some playground equipment for the new park, but they weren't ready to place the equipment in the park yet. The equipment was stored in the shop until it could be put to use in the park. One of the park workers came to Candy and said, "Did you know the playground equipment has disappeared? "

Candy said, "No, what do you mean disappeared? "

"I was driving by that new daycare, and our equipment is in their yard. I know it's ours. Ours mysteriously disappeared from the shop, and the next day it mysteriously appeared at the daycare. "

"Well, I wonder how they got it? "

"I didn't want to say anything, but I stopped in the daycare and asked how they got it. They said Larry gave it to them. "

"Oh no! We paid $8,000.00 for that stuff. "

After the employee left, Candy called Larry. "Hey Larry, people know you gave that playground equipment away. This could be bad. "

Larry stammered and stuttered, then finally said, "Well the day care is a learning center so it should be okay. "

"I don't think so, but let's just hope this don't go any farther. "

***

Larry went by the location of the 'park-to-be', and some city workers were there. Larry, trying to be the almighty in charge, told the workers to have sod put on the whole thing. He told Ivan, the new park dept. supervisor, to go ahead and

After All is Said and Done....More is Said Than Done

get the sod delivered.

A couple of days later Chester saw the sod being laid. He jumped all over Ivan.

"What do you think you're doing? Who authorized you to spend that kind of money?"

Ivan said, "Hold on man, Larry told us to do this."

Chester's face was red, his hands were shaking.

"Ivan don't you ever do anything Larry says again unless you know it is approved by the council."

Chester stormed off. He went to city hall and told Candy to get Larry on the phone. Candy called Larry on his cell. No answer. She called his office only to receive a recorded message. Chester told Candy that when she got hold of Larry, to tell him that he needed to call him.

Later in the day Larry called Candy. "Hey babe, what's up?" Candy rolled her eyes. Same ol' smooth talking Larry.

"Hey Larry, Chester needs you to call him. He's pretty hot about that sod at the park."

Larry got quiet. He said, "Okay, I'll call him."

The next night was the city council meeting. Chester came by city hall that morning on his way to work. He told Candy that Larry never did call him. He said, "He better watch out, cause tonight me and him are gettin some things straight."

Candy, being the peace maker that she was, said, "Now Chester, don't show out tonight."

Chester arrived at city hall early for the council meeting.

"Candy, I talked to my wife about what I was going to say to Larry tonight. She told me not to come down here and embarrass her."

Candy smiled and said, "Ya know Chester that was good advice."

At the council meeting, Chester didn't say a word about

the sod. Larry had gotten by with another one. Seemed like that was always the case. That's probably why he kept doing things that he knew he shouldn't. He knew that no one would actually call him to the carpet.

Chapter 6

With Pat gone from the Police Department, that left the Town with one officer, - Police Chief Nathan McCoy. The City Council decided that since Nathan would be retiring soon, maybe they should go ahead and hire two officers *'since they had all these applications to look at.'*

The City Council decided that Larry and Chester would conduct interviews. They went through all the applications, picked out a few people that they thought would work out well in the town of Hereford, then told Candy to set up some interviews.

On the day of interviews Candy ushered the lucky candidates into the back office one by one to meet with Larry and Chester. One of the applicants was Carter Duncan. Candy had known Carter for many years. They had attended high school together. She asked Carter to have a seat

"They'll be with you in just a few minutes Carter. They're just finishing up on another interview."

Carter nervously sat down in the chair that Candy offered. Neither of them said anything for a few minutes. Candy continued to do her work, and then Carter spoke.

"Candy, I'm really nervous about this. Do you think I have a chance at this job since I'm not a certified police officer?"

Candy replied, "Oh, I think so. We'll send you through CLEET training if you're hired." But really Candy was thinking - they won't hire him.

They chatted a little more while Carter waited his turn. They talked about old friends from school. Laughed about some of the silly things they remembered. It was good to talk to an old acquaintance.

The next day Larry called Candy and told her they were hiring Carter, and a guy named David Hughes. He asked Candy to call both of them and ask them to start work in two weeks. Candy would need to schedule physicals for both of them, and get all of their new employee paperwork done.

David had been a police officer in Tennessee. He had moved back to a neighboring town where he was raised, and his family still lived. Candy could relate to that.

David seemed to have a lot of experience in law enforcement. He had worked in Memphis, which was going to be quite a change to the sleepy town of Hereford. Larry asked David in his interview if he could slow down to Hereford's pace. "We really only need a night watchman here. There isn't really any crime in Hereford." David assured Larry that he would love the slower pace. Since David was a certified police officer in Tennessee he wouldn't have any trouble going through a short refresher course in CLEET (Council of Law Enforcement Education and Training) to be certified in Oklahoma.

Candy spoke with David and he was very excited. Candy thought he was a really nice, polite person. She was going to like David.

She then called Carter. She knew Carter from high school, but they were never in the same circle. Carter was an athlete, and the girls liked him a lot. Candy was always very quiet. Even though she was in all the school clubs, she had her one little group of girls that she hung around with. Carter on the other hand was *'the man'* so to speak. Not the case anymore. Carter was overweight, and his looks had changed dramatically. People who knew him then, and hadn't seen him since high school, wouldn't recognize him now. His hair was prematurely gray - what little hair he had anyway, and he weighed 270 pounds. Not the ladies' man he used to be.

After All is Said and Done....More is Said Than Done

Candy had a little bit of the '*serves-him-right*' attitude.

Carter was also very excited about going to work in Hereford. He had lived there most of his life, and it would be so good to be working right here at home.

Candy scheduled both of the guy's physicals. Carter seemed a little nervous about taking the physical, but Candy didn't think too much about it. A lot of people were scared of doctors after all. He was probably nervous about his weight, but according to the City Council, that wasn't a problem. Since there wasn't any real crime in Hereford, Carter wouldn't be chasing after anyone on foot, or even in a car for that matter.

After their physicals were taken and all was well, Candy enrolled them in CLEET training. David would go first.

***

Nathan was a fit man of 64 years and 6 months. He was counting the days until he could retire. He had a calendar marking off the days till retirement. Every day he would go into city hall and announce how many days he had left to work. "Just ...... more days."

Nathan really liked David. David and Nathan's dad had known each other for many years, so the connection was already established before David went to work for the town of Hereford. David was tall, over six feet. Not too heavy, not to slim. He had sandy blond hair and dark blue eyes that could stare right through you. Nathan wanted David to be the next Chief of Police for the town of Hereford, and David was glad to step in.

On the other hand, Nathan didn't like Carter very much. He remembered him from his high school days as a smart mouth kid, and he was determined to outcast Carter. "He'll never make it through CLEET David. After he's gone we'll find someone else that you want to work here."

David was pleased that he was Nathan's pick. This was a perfect gig for him. The pay was decent and he was going to be in charge. David really knew how to work Nathan too. Even though he was plotting to get rid of Carter all along, he let Nathan think it was all up to him.

David looked innocently at Nathan and said, "Well, whatever you think Nathan. If you don't like Carter I'll do whatever you want me to do."

"You're a top notch officer David and I don't want some idiot like Carter working here. You don't need that. You need someone here who you can count on in a crisis after I'm gone. I just can't believe the city council hired him in the first place."

While David was away at CLEET training, Carter worked nights, while Nathan worked days. They didn't have to cross paths very often, but Nathan kept close watch on Carter. Nathan listened to his police scanner at night to hear what Carter was up to.

Nathan told Carter, "Don't write any tickets while you're out there. You don't have the qualifications or experience to be out there working anyway. Just drive around and make sure everyone in town is safe. That's all you need to be doing right now. And don't use a lot of gas. Find a place to park where you'll be seen by the town folks and stay out of stuff! I don't want people calling me complaining about you."

Carter didn't really understand why Nathan didn't like him, but oh well, he would just lay low.

The county dispatcher called Carter on his radio one night and asked him to watch for a vehicle last seen headed toward Hereford. A county deputy had attempted to stop the vehicle and it ran. Carter was excited and nervous. Nathan had given him strict instructions not to leave the city limits. Carter was sitting in his police unit just at the edge of Hereford city limits when he saw the vehicle that the county radioed him about. Carter immediately turned on his lights and siren and went after the vehicle. The chase was on.

Carter got on his radio and told the county he was in pursuit. Nathan was furious as he listened. Nathan got on the phone with a couple of his State Trooper buddies and told them that if Carter called them for backup to "kind of hang low". Nathan said, "I don't want him to get hurt, but I do want him to learn a lesson."

"Sure thing Nathan. We'll be close in case he really needs us."

The chase immediately headed to the woods outside of Hereford. Carter was right behind the suspects. Carter got back on his radio and called for backup. The Troopers immediately answered his call. "What's your 10/20 Hereford 3?"

With a trembling hand and a shaky voice, Carter carefully spoke his location into the microphone.

The Trooper responded, "I'm not sure of your 10/20 Hereford 3. Repeat that location."

"I'm just past the west side of the Hereford city limits, go left at the county line road, go a mile then turn right, I'm approximately a quarter of mile after you turn right. I'm still in pursuit."

The police scanner was on at Candy's house too. She and Pat were listening to the whole thing. They knew exactly where Carter was, and they couldn't figure out why the Trooper was confused about Carter's directions.

Carter kept giving directions to his location to the Trooper, and he kept saying he didn't know where Carter was. Then the suspects' car crashed, and the two people inside the car bailed out and ran. Carter, still on his radio, informed anyone who would listen, "The vehicle has crashed! The vehicle has crashed! Two suspects are running!" Carter jumped out of his car and ran over to the abandoned vehicle. There was no way he was going to chase them. He wasn't in good physical condition like the two fellas who just jumped out of the abandoned car. The Troopers showed up at the scene just a few minutes behind Carter, but the suspects were long gone.

Carter kind of suspected that the Trooper had really known his location all along, but he didn't want to believe that anyone would do something like that to him. After all, he was *'Carter Duncan the all American athlete'.*

The next day Nathan and Carter had a little chat - so to speak. That is if you can call Nathan screaming and yelling at Carter a chat.

"Why didn't you tell dispatch you couldn't chase after that car and to send someone else! I told you not to leave the city limits! You better not ever do anything like that again. This is your only warning. You got it?"

"Yes sir" was all Carter could say.

Carter was thinking, I'll be glad to get through CLEET. Then Nathan will give me some slack. But that didn't happen.

After All is Said and Done....More is Said Than Done

Chapter 7

The time had finally come for Nathan to retire. Six long months that Carter had listened to Nathan try to tear him down. David and Carter had both made it through CLEET, and with Nathan's recommendation to the city council, David would now be the Chief of Police.

A big retirement sendoff party was planned for Nathan. David went to Candy one day and said, "Candy will you help me organize a surprise retirement party for Nathan."

"Sure David. I'd love to help."

Candy was actually quite good at planning parties, decorating, and such. She was kind of excited to do it.

The party plans were all made. Nathan didn't have a clue. The community center was reserved for the party, and some important people said they would be there. A Senator, a State Representative, lots of local business people, the President of the college, and of course all of the City Council members. David had programs printed and name cards made for the guests of honor. It was going to be a very nice party that Nathan deserved after 27 years on the job.

David called Nathan the morning of the party and told him that he wasn't feeling well.

"Nathan will you work a couple of hours for me tonight. I'm not feeling to good, and I'd like to come in a little late if that's okay."

"Sure David. I'll fill in for you. If you don't get to feeling better just let me know. I can work a split shift or something. "

"Thanks a lot Nathan, I really appreciate it."

That afternoon Candy and David snuck over to the community center to do all the finishing touches. They had it all planned on how to get Nathan over there. After everyone had arrived for the party, David called Nathan and told him that he had received a call that there was a disturbance at a party at the community center.

"Nathan I'm on my way down there right now, but can you go ahead and go over there. I'll be right behind you. After we get this taken care of, you can go on home and I'll work the rest of the shift."

"No problem David, I'm on my way."

Nathan walked into the community center ready to take someone to jail for disturbing the peace, when in fact he found a room full of people yelling "SURPRISE!" Of course Larry had to make a speech, and act like it was all his idea. A few other people gave short speeches, and Nathan was given a very nice engraved law enforcement watch that David had picked out for him. After the speeches were made, and the gift presentation was done, everyone mingled and visited with Nathan. People told him how much he would be missed, and to stay in touch. Candy walked over to Nathan and hugged him lightly.

"Nathan, I don't know if you know it or not, but David was the one who put all this together for you."

"I kind of figured that maybe he did. He's a really good boy. He'll do a good job as Chief. He's almost like a son to me."

That was the first time Candy had seen Nathan so soft hearted.

And so another big change for the Town of Hereford. A new Police Chief would have his own ideas about how to run things. Carter knew he would be fired soon if David had his way. Nathan had made his working at Hereford pretty miserable, but that was nothing compared to what David had in store for him.

Chapter 8

Things were pretty quiet for a while. David got all the paperwork in order for the police department. Nathan wasn't very good at doing the office part of his job. Actually, he just didn't see any need to do it. David got a lot of stuff caught up that Nathan had let go for a long time. Uniform Crime reports had been signed and sent in with none of the information done correctly. The state reported crime based on the UCR reports, and Hereford appeared to be the safest place in the state. In reality drugs were a big problem. Since the police were supposed to only be "night watchmen" things were really getting out of hand. People were being burglarized all the time, a report would be taken and filed in a drawer. The city council liked the way Nathan ran things. He acted like there wasn't any real criminal activity in Hereford. Not only did he act like there was no criminal activity, he reported it to the state that way.

After David got things organized in the police department, he started working. He got to know some of the guys who worked for the county, and they offered to help him. He did it all very carefully though. He made some arrests for drugs, but of course he made sure it was people on the wrong side of the tracks that he got. He caught some burglars trying to break into a church. He got a lot of hallelujahs over that one. People really liked him.

Carter was in the background trying to hang onto his job. He worked the night shift so he wasn't seen very much. David was always pretty nice to Carter, but there was just something about the way he made Carter look like an idiot. He did it in a way that you didn't realize what he was doing.

Even though Carter appeared to be quiet, and just minding his own business, he had his own agenda. He was laying ground to get rid of David. He was working people in town too. He tried to play the role of mentor and counselor to people. He pretended to be everyone's best friend.

There was a girl who had recently been released from prison who made it as far as Hereford and was staying in the local motel. She met Carter at the local truck stop one night. She had gone in to get coffee and decided to sit at the booth to drink it. Carter came in to pay for gas and saw her sitting by herself. He walked over to her table and said, "Everything okay for you tonight mam?"

She was your typical parolee type. She looked rough around the edges. She had stringy long brown hair, kind of skinny, with a couple of jail house tattoos. She was wearing an old pair of jeans and a T-shirt that said *'After All Is Said and Done - More is Said Than Done'*.

"Yep, I'm doin all right. How bout you?"

Carter took that as an invitation to sit down. They introduced themselves.

"I'm Carter. I work for the local police department."

"Hey Carter, I'm Amanda."

He asked her about herself, and she was happy to have someone to talk to, even though he was a cop. She thought he didn't really act much like a cop though. Usually cops were bossy and looking to find you doing something wrong, whether you were or not. But Carter was different. He was pretty charming in fact. She spilled her heart out to him.

"I'm so tired of just tryin to make it. My family is all in Kansas and I'm stuck here. I don't have the money to go home. I can't find a job. Nobody will hire a convict. It's just hard ya know."

After All is Said and Done....More is Said Than Done

Carter looked at her with sympathetic eyes.

"Yes, I'm sure it's tough on you, but maybe I can help. Let me talk to the store manager here and see if I can help get you a job."

Amanda just couldn't believe it. A cop offering to help her. Nobody else in this town had even spoken to her. This meant she may be able to get enough money soon to get out of that motel room she was staying in, and head to Kansas.

Carter couldn't wait to tell David about this good deed he had done. David would be jealous, and wish he had done something like this to get brownie points. The next day Carter told David about meeting Amanda.

"You better be careful Carter. The city council don't like people with her background living in Hereford." David said. "It's good that you got her the job though. Maybe she can get her first paycheck and get on a bus to Kansas."

Amanda started calling Carter every time she got lonely or depressed, which was nightly. Carter would talk to her and assure her that her life was going to get better. He told her that he was her friend, and to call him any time she wanted. Well she did just that. She usually called him while she was at work. She had the night shift and so did Carter, so that made it convenient to talk to him.

David was closely watching everything that Carter did. Even his phone log. He saw that Carter was having frequent conversations with Amanda. It had to be her. Who else would he talk to at the truck stop?

David asked Carter, "How's Amanda doing? You ever talk to her?"

Carter had no clue that David already knew he had been talking to Amanda.

"She's doing okay I guess. She's kind of having a hard time

adjusting, and she calls me a lot. I sure feel sorry for her, but she'll get through this."

David came up with a great idea to embarrass Carter. Carter's birthday was coming up, and he had a plan. David hadn't told anyone about Amanda. He didn't want anybody getting the idea that Carter may be a nice guy.

"Let's see, his birthday is Thursday. I've been thinking about this Candy. There is this girl that calls Carter all the time because she thinks he's her counselor, if you can imagine that. We'll get the office decorated a little, get a cake, and invite a few people, and then you call Carter and tell him there is some girl in the bathroom crying who says the only one she will talk to is him. I'll get someone to hide in the bathroom in a crazy costume, and when Carter thinks he has talked her into coming out of the bathroom - SURPRISE!" David said.

Candy was already laughing at the thought of it. She was thinking, what a good guy David is, he's always doing something for someone.

Everything went just as planned.

On the day of the party, Candy called Carter. In a whispered voice she said, "Carter, there's a girl down here at city hall. She's locked herself in the bathroom and says she's not coming out. She said you're the only one she will talk to. You better get down here."

"I'll be right there!"

David was standing by Candy's desk when she made the phone call. They were both trying not to laugh. When Candy hung up the phone they burst out laughing. Most of the employees were there to celebrate the birthday. They all went into one of the back rooms and closed the door so Carter wouldn't see them when he came in. The only ones in the outer office were David and Candy.

After All is Said and Done....More is Said Than Done

Carter was practically running when he came through the door of city hall. He didn't even look at Candy. He went straight to the bathroom where David was standing, pretending to try to reason with the girl. David whispered "She says she's going to kill herself." Carter never even noticed the birthday decorations behind him. "Hun, it's me, Carter." Then he heard the girl sobbing. "Carter I just hate it here. I want to see my family. I'm never going to be able to get enough money to go home." Carter was so nervous his hands were shaking. He was thinking, *'that girl may have a gun'*. He put his hand on his revolver just in case she came out shooting. He continued to talk to her for a few minutes. Trying to reassure her that her life was going to get better. She said, "Carter, if you could have just one wish, what would it be?" Carter seemed a little confused by her question, but he said, "Well Hun, my wish would be for you to come out of that bathroom." He heard the lock on the door turn. Then the door knob started to turn. Carter moved to the side of the door, hand on his gun, and trembling. Music started playing in the background and people started coming out of the back office. Carter's mind was spinning. *'Oh my gosh, they're giving me a birthday party. I've got to get these people out of here. Of all times to have a party. I'm dealing with a suicidal girl here'*. Carter started franticly waving his hand at the people coming out of the back office. He whispered angrily "get back - get back!!!" About that time a young pretty girl in a genie costume walked out of the bathroom doing a little dance, and said "Happy birthday Carter". The poor guy almost fainted. It's a wonder they didn't have to call the paramedics.

David was ecstatic. Everyone laughed for years about the way Carter looked when that girl came out of the bathroom. Carter on the other hand, didn't think it was so funny. David would get his.

Chapter 9

A few months went by unnoticed. The silent battle between David and Carter continued. And all was well in the Town of Hereford. David was cleaning up the drug activity and making a lot of friends. Carter was also making friends by offering to be EVERYONE's friend, so to speak.

Although David knew he had the upper hand, he still had to get rid of Carter. He didn't like Carter one bit. David did everything he could to make sure the City council knew how valuable he was to the town. He found out about a grant for the police department that would pay for another officer. This would work. He would get the grant, hire another officer, get him through CLEET, and then the two of them would find a way to get rid of Carter.

With help from Candy, they got the grant application sent in, and were awarded enough money to pay a new officers salary and benefits. David already had someone in mind for the job. Josh Simpleton was hired and sent to CLEET training, while David and Carter held down the fort.

David decided that while Josh was away at training, he would give it one more try to like Carter. He thought that maybe if he just spent some time with him, they could work out their personality differences.

"Hey Carter, wanna go with me to do some target practice Saturday morning?" David asked.

Carter just couldn't believe that David would ask him to do something with him.

"You mean go to the firing range?" asked Carter.

"No, I thought we'd just go out to the old coal pits and shoot at some cans. Nobody ever goes out there. What do ya say?"

"I guess so. I'm not sure if my wife has anything planned for Saturday morning or not. Let me check first. What time do you want to go?"

"Let's go early. Say around six in the morning."

"Okay, I'll let ya know."

The more Carter thought about it, the more strange this all seemed. He decided that going out in the middle of nowhere with David and a loaded gun, may not be the best idea. Carter's paranoia was working overtime. He later told David that he couldn't go.

David seemed disappointed. "Well another time then."

"Sure, another time." was all Carter could say. He just knew that David had something up his sleeve.

David came by and talked to Candy pretty often. She noticed that David was becoming obsessed with trying to convince her that Carter wasn't a stable person, and that he shouldn't be carrying a gun. Sometimes it even frightened Candy by the look in David's eyes when he'd talk about Carter.

David became so frustrated that he couldn't convince people that Carter was dangerous. He decided that he wasn't sticking around any longer. He called Larry and said "I have to quit this job Larry. I have some things that I need to straighten out in my personal life."

It was all so sudden that Larry wasn't prepared to talk David into staying.

"Well, okay David. When are you leaving us?"

"Today. Today will be my last day. I'll turn all my stuff in to Candy."

"Man, I hope everything works out okay for you David. Is there anything I can do to help?"

"No. I need to work this out on my own. Thanks though."

Larry called Candy and told her about his conversation

with David. She really hated for David to quit, but she knew if she hated working with someone as much as David hated Carter, she'd quit too.

When word got out that David had quit, Carter was ecstatic. He immediately went to each of the City Council members to assure them that he was fully capable of being the next Police Chief.

Larry called a special meeting and the council unanimously voted to make Carter the Police Chief. Carter called a friend of his who worked for the newspaper, and the next day a story with a big picture of Carter was on the front page of the paper. A big banner across the top of the paper read "HOME TOWN BOY IS THE NEW CHIEF OF POLICE".

Chester laughed as he read the paper to his wife that morning. "He'd work for free as long as people call him Chief".

Chester didn't like Carter. There was just something about him. And besides, he was still angry about Pat leaving.

Carter cut the story out of the paper and started a scrap book. He knew there would be many more stories about him in the Herford Journal. He'd make sure of that.

Chapter 10

It had been four years since David left and Carter had become the Chief of Police. There had been a couple of council members who didn't file for re-election so that meant getting use to new council members. Chester didn't file for re-election. He was finally tired of dealing with Larry, and Carter, and just the whole big picture.

New council members always came in thinking they could change everything, and then they would find out that they couldn't.

Problems had started with Rita again. She came into work late every day. She had started taking afternoon naps again, and what little work she did was not done in a timely manner. Candy usually opened the mail every day. She got a notice from the Corp of Engineers that the water reports that Rita was supposed to do hadn't been done for months. The auditors came to do the annual audit, and found that the bank statements had not been reconciled since the audit the previous year.

Rita knew she wasn't doing her job well anymore. She was tired and ready to slow down. She asked the city council if she could start working part-time. The city council agreed to let her start working a couple of days a week and they told Candy to advertise for help. They also told Candy that she would have to start doing a lot of the work that Rita should have been doing. Candy didn't really want the added work load. Actually she was afraid she may not be able to do some of the things Rita was supposed to do. Apparently Rita couldn't do it.

Candy spent a couple of days working with Rita, trying to learn what it was she did, but that just wasn't going to work out. From what Candy could figure out, Rita's books were a mess. She got on the phone and contacted the people who provided the computer software for the town, and asked them to send someone down to train her. They sent a guy down who worked with Candy for a week. He said that what little Rita had done, was not done right, and that Candy was going to have her hands full getting it all straightened out. It took Candy months to get all the data in the computer. She worked long hours, prayed about it a lot, and felt good about herself when it was finally done.

Rita on the other hand, was basically doing nothing but coming into the office sixteen hours a week and reading magazines.

After Rita started working part time, the City Council hired a woman named Marla Overton to work in the office. Candy just loved her. They hit it off right from the start.

"Oh Lord, I just realized its "R" day. " Candy said.

That's what they called it on the days that Rita was going to be there.

With a little moan, Marla rolled her eyes and said, "I was just thinking the same thing. I dread coming to work when she's gonna be here. You can just feel the tension in this place."

"I know it. I have to bite my tongue all day. One of these days it's going to get ugly I'm afraid."

And today was that day.

After All is Said and Done....More is Said Than Done

Chapter 11

"Where do you want us to put this pop machine Mam?" the distributor asked Candy.

"Just put it in the front lobby please. There are electrical outlets right beside that little table."

Rita came storming over to Candy's desk.

"We had a soda machine in here one time before and it was the biggest mess!"

Candy ignored her but her temper was flaring.

Rita just couldn't let it go. She said, "Did the Council say you could put that in here?"

Candy turned and looked at Rita with fire in her eyes. With a low voice, and her teeth gritted, she said slowly, "Rita, this is none of your business, and you need to turn around and go right back over there to your desk before you really make me mad."

Rita tear'd up a little, and in a really high pitched voice said, "Well, I didn't mean to make you mad" as she stormed off.

Marla was sitting quietly at her desk. After Rita was out of ear shot she said, "I knew she was gonna push you to far one of these days."

That was just the straw that broke the camel's back. Candy called Larry and told him that she needed to meet with him. He told her that he would be by when he got off work. Candy told him that she would be there waiting for him.

"Larry I just can't take it anymore. I have put up with her for six years now and that's just all I have in me."

"I'll talk to her in the morning. I don't know why we've let it go this long."

Sure enough, Larry actually did what he said he'd do. He showed up at city hall at 8:30 the next morning. He told Candy that he had called Rita and asked her to come to city hall to talk to him.

"I'll be in the back office when she comes in. Tell her to come back there."

"Okay. I don't know what the answer is Larry, but Marla and Me are about to go crazy here."

"I know, so is the city council."

Rita showed up and Candy told her that Larry was waiting for her. She went into the back office and closed the door. About an hour later Rita came out of the back office and left city hall. Larry asked Candy to come into the back office.

"I kind of gave her an ultimatum to quit or be fired. I told her that if she'd quit we'd pay her for all her built up sick leave and vacation. She jumped all over it."

"Holy Moly! I didn't think you were going to fire her. I thought you'd probably just tell her that she needed to quit minding everyone's business but her own."

"I'd do anything for you babe, and I know you wanted her out of your hair."

The real truth was that Larry was sick of dealing with her at the council meetings and anytime he came into city hall, but he knew Candy would believe that he did it for her.

***

Marla and Candy just loved working together. After Rita left, things were so much more pleasant. It was really fun to come to work. Marla and Candy had so much in common. They liked the same things, and had the same work habits. It was almost like they could read each other's minds.

They became the best of friends. They planned big dinners for all of the employees at Thanksgiving and Christmas. They

After All is Said and Done....More is Said Than Done

joined the Chamber of Commerce, and before they knew what they had gotten into they were officers. They worked non-stop the first year they were in the Chamber of Commerce. They did everything they could to help with every project. They just worked so well together in everything they did, but nothing lasts forever.

Chapter 12

Audrey Meadows had fixed her daughter Candy lunch now every day since she started working at Hereford City Hall. And every day when Candy walked in the door of her Mom and Dad's house for lunch she would say, "Hey Pop, what's for lunch today?" And no matter what it was that Audrey had fixed, Candy would say, "Alright! I love meatloaf"… or hamburgers, or roast beef, or whatever it was.

Today the computer guy had come to Hereford city hall to update the system.

"Candy do you want to go to lunch somewhere? I'm buying", said the tech.

"No thanks, I go to my Mom's every day. She'll be expecting me."

Candy, and her Mom and Dad, had just sat down to eat lunch when the doorbell rang. Audrey went to the door. It was Carter. Candy's Mom was such a sweetheart. She told Carter to come in.

"I don't want to interrupt your lunch Mrs. Meadows. I just needed to ask Candy about something."

"No, no, you're not bothering us. Come on in."

Carter followed Audrey into the kitchen.

Candy said, "Hi Carter. Sit down. Have some lunch with us."

"Oh no, that's okay."

"We have plenty. Mom's feelings will be hurt if you don't join us."

"Well….., if you're sure."

Everyone liked Candy's Mom and Dad. They were "just good hard working people" everyone would say. Lots of

After All is Said and Done....More is Said Than Done

people were friends with Mr. and Mrs. Meadows. Audrey was known for her homemade cinnamon rolls and bread. She did volunteer work at the Country Manor nursing home, and taught Sunday school. Herb was the town's best small engine repair man. Both were retired, but they stayed very busy.

After they had finished their lunch, Carter thanked Audrey. Audrey told him to come any time. He was always welcome in their home.

As Carter and Candy were walking out the front door to go back to work, Candy asked, "Carter, did you need something? You said you stopped by to ask me something. "

Carter smiled and said, "I don't even remember what it was now Candy. " Then they both laughed.

They had a nice visit. Carter almost felt ashamed about some of the things he had been saying to people about Candy. She and her family were such nice people. But he was so paranoid all the time that he started thinking they were just nice to him for some underlying motive.

After All is Said and Done....
More is Said Than Done

PART 2

After All is Said and Done....More is Said Than Done

Chapter 13

As the years came and went, so did employees. There was always turnover but Candy use to jokingly say "I guess I'll be here till I die." She had been working for the town of Hereford now for 14 years.

There were a couple of other diehard employees. Carter and Larry, a street dept. worker, and a young man named Adam Johnson, who worked in the water department.

Adam Johnson started as summer help just a couple of months after Candy started working for the town. He was only 18 years old at the time. He happened to be in the right place at the right time, and was quickly moved into a supervisory position. He was good at his job. He was smart. And he deserved to be where he was. Over the years Candy became friends with Carter and Adam. She knew that Carter always had motives for what he did. Motives for his own good, but still they were friends. Pat told her all the time, "You better watch out with him Candy. He's a snake in the grass, just waiting to strike. "

Adam, on the other hand, didn't hold anything back. He had a violent temper. People could tell him things that other employees said about him. He'd believe every word, even if the words were taken out of context, and have a raging fit. Candy always tried to calm him down and make peace.

Carter was an instigator of problems with the employees. He did it in a carefully calculated manner. He played the role of best friend to everyone, but in reality he was stirring the pot all the time. And he was quite good at it.

Candy's children were grown up now. Abby was in college, and Cale was a senior in high school. Candy was so proud of her kids. She had been praying for them their whole lives, and God had watched over them. They were good kids. People told Candy all the time what a great job she had done in raising them, but Candy always gave that glory to God. She told people many times, "I couldn't have done it by myself. God led me every step of the way."

Carter was very jealous of the fact that Candy's kids were so highly regarded. Even more jealous of the fact that people mentioned it to Candy all the time.

It was time for the Seniors of Hereford High School to go on the annual senior trip. This group of kids had been working since they were freshman in high school to raise money. They had car washes, bake sales, garage sales, and anything else they could think of for fund raisers. They had raised enough money to take a trip to Dallas Texas. They were going to a Cowboys football game, and Six Flags amusement park. Cale got his things all packed and ready to go. Candy had mixed emotions about it. She asked God once again to keep his angels watching over Cale while he was away. Jokingly Candy said, "Now don't you get into any trouble while you're down there. I don't want to have to come down there and get you."

Cale just grinned and said, "I won't".

"I'll miss you. Have a good time. BUT DON'T get into any trouble." Candy hugged Cale and off he went.

***

Cale returned home from the trip safely. He had a good time while he was away. He talked about the football game a lot.

"We'll have to go to a game sometime Mom. You would love it."

"Maybe we'll go to a Kansas City game. I bet your Papa would want to go with us."

"That would be great! I'll talk to Papa about it. I know he and Mama would go. Hey Mom, did you hear about Chad and Trent getting into a little trouble while we were in Dallas?"

"Nooooo, I did not. What happened?"

Cale kind of laughed like he was thinking about what had happened. "They had some handcuffs and put them on Chucky Barton. They didn't have a key to get em off. Chucky was screaming for help and Coach Parker heard him, and came runnin in to see what was wrong. They had to call the police to get the cuffs unlocked."

Cale was laughing so hard he nearly had tears. Candy was laughing too. She said, "Did you have anything to do with it?" Cale, still giggling, said, "nooooooo."

A few days later at the office Candy was telling Marla about what Cale had told her. Carter and Adam were in the office too. Carter said, "Come back here a minute Candy. I need to tell you something." Marla gave Carter a look that would kill. Candy and Carter went into the back office.

"Candy, I hate to be the one to tell you this, but you're my friend, and I don't want you to be in the dark." He hesitated like he felt so badly about what he was about to tell her.

Candy said, "Okay Carter, what did Cale do." She knew it had to be something about Cale since she was just talking about what the boys had done on senior trip.

Carter looked pained, and said, "The handcuffs were Pat's. Cale took them on the trip."

"Oh really." Candy said with aggravation in her voice. "I guess me and Cale are going to have a talk tonight."

Carter and Candy talked a little more, than walked back out into the front office. Adam was gone and Marla was fuming, but she kept her mouth shut.

Candy went to the post office, and while she was gone

Marla told Carter what she thought.

"You shouldn't have told Candy about that. You know that's going to cause some problems for her and Cale, and it wasn't your place to tell her. That is a matter between her and him, and you're sticking your nose into personal business that you don't need to be in."

"She's my friend Marla! I didn't want her telling anyone else about that unless she knew the whole story. Friends are supposed to be there for each other, and I did it to protect her from being embarrassed by not knowing."

"You did not. You can tell her that all day long Carter, but you and I both know you told her that to get Cale in trouble. You can't stand it because people love her kids."

As Carter was walking out the door, he said, "That's not true Marla. I did it because I care about Candy."

When Candy got back to the office Marla told her about her conversation with Carter, but she didn't give her details. She just said that she told Carter he should mind his own business.

After Candy got home from work Carter called her.

"Candy is everything okay?" Candy started to cry.

"Thanks for telling me about it Carter. You know, it's not what Cale did, it's that he lied to me. My feelings are so hurt. Cale isn't home, so I haven't talked to him yet."

"I'm so sorry Candy. You know I only told you about it because you're my friend, and friends are supposed to take care of each other."

"I know. It's okay. I'm glad you told me."

"Marla is really mad at me for telling you. I don't want you to be mad at me."

"It's okay. Really."

Candy was waiting on the front porch for Cale when he got home. He said "Hey Mom, what cha doin?"

After All is Said and Done....More is Said Than Done

Candy had tears in her eyes. "Cale I'm so hurt because you lied to me about the handcuffs. I just want you to know that."

Cale looked so sad. "I'm sorry Mom. How did you find out?"

"That really don't matter, but Carter told me. I guess everyone in town knew but me."

Cale hated that he had hurt his Mother. His heart was broken too. He walked into the house. A few minutes later he walked back out onto the porch where Candy was and said, "Mom, I'll never lie to you again."

Candy looked at him and said "Okay Cale, I believe you." And it was over and done. That is with Cale anyway. Carter was a different story.

Chapter 14

It was the worst time of Candy's life. She felt pain like she had never felt. Pain that she didn't think was possible to live through.

Herb and Audrey Meadows died within two months of each other. They had been married sixty-three years. Audrey was fifteen and Herb was 23 when they got married.

Neither of them went through long terminal illnesses, and there wasn't a tragic accident. Audrey died from a sudden heart attack. Some say that Herb died from old age symptoms. He was 86 years old. But the truth was that he died of grief for Audrey. And now Candy's life would never be the same.

The funerals were huge, but Candy didn't really see or hear any of it. The church held more flowers than Hereford had ever seen. The line of cars leaving the church, and going out to the cemetery, strung for three miles. But Candy was oblivious to it all.

Over the next few months every time Candy closed her eyes to sleep she saw her Mom and Dad. She saw them in the casket. She saw them at the hospital. She saw them, and she cried.

The next year was a blur. Days went by. Life went on. But Candy wasn't the same. She cried when she woke up in the mornings, and she cried when she went to bed at night. She missed her Mom and Dad. The house that Candy grew up in sat empty like her heart.

Pat was so caring and patient. He worried over Candy. He gave her space and time to heal, but he was always there if she needed him.

Chapter 15

After Candy's Mom passed away, her Dad asked her if she wanted their cabin at the lake. He said he just couldn't spend time there without Audrey.

Candy bought the lake property from Herb. It was a piece of her Mother that she could hold onto.

Candy liked spending time at the cabin. Pat -- not so much. He said it was too noisy. Too many boats and jet skis, and way too many people for his country spirit.

Candy wanted to spend time with her brothers and sisters. She didn't want to ever lose the closeness they had. They were a part of her life that she just had to hang onto. Life was too short. She knew that if Audrey and Herb had lived to be 100, it still wouldn't have been enough days with them.

Chapter 16

As time went by, Candy was coming to terms with her Mom and Dad being gone. She pulled herself up off the floor and told herself that she had to be strong for her kids. Audrey wouldn't want her to let them down.

The first week that Candy didn't go to Audrey's for lunch was torture. Candy talked to all of the city employees and asked them if they would like to start taking thirty minutes for lunch instead of an hour. They could go home thirty minutes earlier. They all really liked that idea. Candy really didn't want to take an hour lunch anymore. That gave her too much time to be sad.

"Hey Larry, I've spoken to all of the employees about cutting our lunch time to thirty minutes and going home at 4:30. Everyone is in favor of it. Could we put it on the agenda to change the business hours?"

"Sure, I guess so."

"With Mom and Dad gone……, well, I just don't know what to do with myself. Most of the time I just eat at my desk."

"I'm so sorry Candy. It will get easier. Go ahead and start the thirty minute lunch thing. I'll talk to the other council members."

"Thanks Larry."

When Candy did leave the office for lunch, she would grab something quick at a drive thru, and take it out to the cemetery to eat. She knew her Mom and Dad weren't in the cemetery. They were both walking the streets of gold in heaven. But she just felt close to them when she was at the cemetery.

As time went by, Larry was right. It did get easier. Candy still went to the cemetery a lot, but when she went, she didn't cry any more. She sat on the bench that she and her brothers and sisters had put by Audrey and Herb's graves. She talked to God, and she asked God questions that she knew she would never have answers for.

Chapter 17

"I've got a doctor's appointment next Wednesday Candy. It's in Tulsa so I won't be in until after noon if that's okay with you." Marla seemed a little stressed lately. She said she just didn't feel good but she just couldn't really pin point what was wrong.

Candy said, "Are you just getting a checkup Marla?"

"Yea, I just feel so tired all the time, my bones ache, and I just think they need to give me the once over. Maybe I'm low on iron or something."

Candy figured there was probably just something simple going on with Marla. Maybe she just needed some vitamins.

Wednesday afternoon Marla called Candy and told her that she wouldn't be in to work. The doctor wanted to run a couple of tests. Nothing to worry about, just routine.

Four days after Marla's doctor appointment Marla and Candy worked and talked as usual, but they both knew that the doctor was supposed to call Marla today with her test results. They were both kind of nervous about it, but they pretended not to be. It was almost 5 o'clock and the doctor still hadn't called. Marla looked at Candy and said, "Why don't you go on home Candy. I'm going to wait here just a little longer because the doctor said he would call me here at the office. I'm afraid if I start home I'll miss his call."

Candy, never looking up from her work, "No, I'm still working on payroll. I'll just hang around too."

At 5:15 the phone rang. It was Doctor McKnight for Marla. Marla and Candy's hearts skipped a beat. Marla took the phone. "Yes…….. Really…………. Okay………. What time? Okay. Thank you, I'll see you tomorrow." Marla hung up the phone and began to cry. Candy was already at her side holding her hand. "Marla can you tell me what he said?" Marla looked at Candy with tears in her eyes and said, "I have to go for more tests tomorrow. He says it's urgent. He thinks I may have cancer." Candy was doing all she could to try to hold back the tears, but it just wasn't working. They held each other and sobbed.

Marla was a trooper. She knew she had to be strong to get through this. She went to the hospital the next morning for more tests with a good attitude. It didn't take long for the doctor to confirm that Marla had breast cancer. She would need surgery right away. Marla called Candy and told her the news. Marla didn't shed a tear. Candy on the other hand was devastated. Marla spoke to Candy like it was no more than a bad cold. "I'm going to be fine. I really don't have any doubt about it. I don't think I'll be able to come back to work though. This just might be a good time for me to retire. You should go ahead and find someone to replace me at the office Candy."

"Maybe you'll feel like coming back after your surgery Marla. Why don't we wait and see?"

"No, I really think I should just go ahead and quit. You go ahead and hire someone. I've been thinking about it, and if I feel up to it later, I might just do some sewing and alterations out of my home. Just a little something to keep me busy. I like the idea of retirement."

"Okay Marla, but if you change your mind, you know you can come back to work here."

Marla had surgery and her recovery was amazing. She didn't have to have chemotherapy or radiation. The doctor said he was amazed at how quickly she recovered. She was cancer free. Candy and Marla knew the reason for Marla's quick recovery. Lots of prayers had been sent to the 'Man In

Charge'.

As bad as Candy hated to replace Marla, she knew it had to be done. She had a few applications but none that she thought would qualify for the position. Then she got a call from Larry. "Hey babe. Do you know Denise Evers? I just heard that she quit her job with the cell phone place. Word is she's lookin for another job."

"Sure, I know her. I always really liked her."

"Why don't you give her a call and see what ya think."

"Okay, I'll do that. I'll let you know after I talk to her."

Candy looked up Denise's phone number and called her. "Hi Denise. This is Candy down at city hall."

"Hi Candy."

"Hey, I heard you may be looking for a job, and I'm looking for someone to replace Marla. I was wondering if you might be interested."

"I sure am."

"Can you come by the office tomorrow afternoon, and we'll visit about it."

"I'd be glad to. Is around 2 o'clock okay."

"That works perfect for me. See ya than."

Candy hung up the phone and called Larry. "Hey Larry, I'm meeting with Denise tomorrow at 2 o'clock."

"Oh good. Let me know how it goes."

"Okie Dokie. I'll talk to you tomorrow then."

The next day Denise and Candy were talking when Carter came into city hall. He walked over to Candy's desk and said, "Hi Denise. How ya doin?"

Denise replied "I'm well. Thank you for asking."

Carter looked at Candy and said, "Mind if I sit in?"

Candy said "No, have a seat."

Carter started doing all the talking. He told Denise about

how much she would like working at city hall. How they were all one big happy family. Denise told them a little bit about her previous job. She certainly had the qualifications Candy was looking for. Candy liked Denise, always had, and she thought Denise really would be a good fit.

So, Candy called Larry and told him what she thought. He said he would put it on the agenda for the next council meeting to hire her. "It's a done deal", Larry said.

And so it was. Denise started to work. Candy loved her. They became best of buddies. And Carter was once again jealous and put out.

Chapter 18

Candy had really stepped up to the plate in her job. She took her job very seriously. She wanted to be good at it, and she was. She continued to study anything she could get her hands on about municipal government. The city council relied on her for all the answers. She joined all the local civic groups so she would be associated with the business people in town. She got to know her County and State legislators. She was elected to the state executive board for the Oklahoma Court Clerks Association. She was a member of the International City Clerks Association. Candy was liked by the people of Hereford, and Candy liked them. No, in fact she loved this little town, and the people in it.

Through Candy's take control attitude, and her association with people in economic development for the State of Oklahoma, she had helped bring progress and change to the Town of Hereford. People were seeing good things happen. There were several new businesses. And with the grants that Candy had been able to get for the town, they had new asphalt on the streets, sidewalks, a new police station, fire department, and emergency medical treatment facility. Candy loved her job.

Candy was away at a conference when she received a call from Carter. "Hey Candy, I know your busy, but I've been talking to Larry, and I think you do way more than a City Clerk. I have him convinced that you need to be made 'City Manager'. I know it's just a title and all, but that's what you really are. The only change I can see would be that you will be in charge of all the employees."

Candy had never even considered a title change. What

difference did it make anyway? "I'll talk to you about it when I get back. What did Larry say about it?"

"He's all for it. He's tired of having to do employee reviews and discipline and that stuff. He said the other council members are too, and if you'd do this it would be great."

"Hmmm, okay, we'll see."

Candy hung up the phone and looked at her friend Pam and said, "That was kind of weird. They want me to be 'City Manager', whatever that means." Pam said, "You're kidding. Like you don't already do enough!"

When Candy got back to work from the conference, Carter couldn't wait to talk to her. He acted like - Look What I'm Doing for You! He said "This will be great Candy. You deserve this. You already do all the work." Candy talked to Larry and he said basically the same thing. Larry said, "And I'll make sure you get a raise." Candy agreed to accept the challenge. And boy what a challenge it was.

According to State Statutes, Council members are not allowed to discuss anything that is going to be on an agenda, prior to the meeting. All discussion is to be done in an open meeting. That was one of the many laws that Hereford City Council didn't abide by. They always called each other and discussed city matters before the council meetings.

Larry called all the council members and talked to them about appointing Candy as City Manager. They all agreed that it was a good idea, so it was put on the agenda for the next meeting.

The meeting was held on March 25th, 2003. The motion was made for Candy to "become city manager and assume extra duties, with her salary to be determined at the next regular meeting". Everyone voted "yes".

Chapter 19

Seemed like Candy's work load just kept growing. She had several grants that she was working on. She spent a lot of time working on economic development too. Denise told Candy that she would start doing the court stuff to take some of the load off of her. Candy was glad to turn it over to her, and Denise seemed to enjoy doing it.

At the next city council meeting, which was the first of April, the city council voted to give Candy and Denise both one-hundred dollar a month raises. They also voted to give Carter one-hundred dollars more a month. They said for added duties. Candy and Denise were a little confused as to what Carter's added duties were, but oh well.

The first thing Candy was hit with after assuming her new duties was Carter tattle telling on everyone. He knew he could rat everyone out, and Candy would never tell where she got the information.

Carter called Candy and said, "I have a problem." He sounded worried. "Can you talk? Can anyone hear you?"

"Yes, I can talk. No one can hear me."

"Gosh, I don't know what to do. Mike has really been hard up." Mike was one of the towns' newest police officers. "He needed some money. I've loaned him money several times, but this time I didn't have any to give him, so I loaned him money out of the drug fund."

The town had a little fund set up for secret investigations, such as drugs. It was set up when David was working there. There was Two-hundred and fifty dollars in the fund. Since David left, Hereford Police never did drug investigations, so none of the money was ever spent. It was cash money sitting in a locked box that only Carter had the key for.

Candy couldn't believe what she was hearing. "I don't have to tell you that's illegal."

In a desperate attempt to justify what he had done, Carter said, "No. I know I shouldn't have done it, but I felt sorry for him. Problem is, he said he'd pay it back last week, and he still hasn't. I've asked him for it, and he says he don't have it." Carter was really sounding nervous now. "What am I going to do?"

With a sigh, Candy said, "I'll call him."

"Oh thank you Candy. Pleeeeease call me back after you talk to him."

"I will."

Candy dialed Mike's number and he answered on the first ring. "Hey Mike. Carter told me about loaning you money from the drug fund. First of all, he shouldn't have. Second it's illegal, and you could both be in a lot of trouble."

Mike didn't say a word. Candy continued. "Carter says you don't have the money to pay back. I don't know how, or where you're going to come up with that money, but I do know that it better be laying on my desk by close of business today, or I'm going to the council. You get it to me today, and nobody knows about this but you, me, and Carter. I don't think you realize how serious this is."

Mike said, "I'm so sorry Candy. You'll have the money today."

Candy called Carter and told him about her conversation with Mike. Carter was still pretty nervous, but he was feeling some relief. He was confident that Mike would come up with the money.

Later that day Mike came to Candy's office and gave her the money. He apologized again, and told her that when Carter gave him the money he didn't know that Carter took it out of the drug fund. He didn't find that out until he wasn't able to pay it back as he had planned. He assured her that he wouldn't have taken the money from Carter if he had known.

***

Adam was becoming a big problem - according to Carter. "Did you know he did …" It went on and on. Adam buddied with another employee in the water department. His name was Ben. Ben just followed Adam around and did whatever he was told to do. When Carter would talk to Candy about Adam and Ben, he called them "dumb and dumber".

Adam and Ben had started spending a lot of time in the police station. Carter was filling their heads with things to turn them against Candy. Then he would call Candy and tell her how stupid the two of them were, and he wished they would stay out of the police station. He asked her if she would do something about it.

Candy was at her desk working on some pretty important documents that she had to get finished, when she received a call from Carter.

"Hey Candy, I have Adam and Ben sitting here in the police station with me, and they're talkin about what could happen to everybody working here if we have a change in council members. They seem to be pretty worried about it."

Candy was very frustrated with how Carter could make a problem for people to worry about, when there wasn't even a problem. Candy replied pretty harshly, "You know what Carter, you need to tell Adam and Ben that if they would stay out of your office and do their jobs, then they wouldn't have to worry about losing their jobs if we get new council members."

Carter anxiously said, "Hold on, hold on, I'm gonna put you on speaker, and you can tell them that okay."

"Fine."

Candy waited a second. She could hear Carter saying - Candy want's to tell you guys something. Then he said "Okay Candy, tell them what you told me." Candy repeated it. Carter said, " Okay, they heard you. Talk to ya later." Then he hung up.

After Carter hung up the phone he looked at Adam and Ben. They were furious. Adams quick temper had him slinging obscenities about Candy, and out the door they went. Carter was grinning from ear to ear. He picked up the phone and called Candy. "Hey, don't want to bother you, but thanks a lot for doing that. Now maybe those two will leave me alone."

***

Adam had developed a really bad attitude. He was neglecting his job, and the town was suffering for it. Candy had been told by Carter that Adam spent a lot of time playing cards and gambling with some contractors while he was at work. He also told her that Adam had quite a collection of *girly magazines* in his desk.

Adam had started being distant with Candy because Carter had made him think that Candy was the bad guy.

Finally Candy talked to Larry about Adam. Larry told her to give Adam an ultimatum. "He better straighten up, or we're going to replace him." Candy really hated to put it to Adam like that, but she had to do what Larry said.

"Adam, I need you to come to my office when you get a minute."

"I'll be right there."

Adam walked into Candy's office and said "What's up?" Candy talked to Adam about the things he had been doing, and not doing. She said, "The Council told me to tell you that if this doesn't stop they will have to find someone else to do your job."

Adam was furious. "So are you firing me?"

"I'm telling you, that if this doesn't stop, they are going to find someone else to do your job."

Adam took the keys that belonged to the city and dropped them on Candy's desk. "There ya go." was all he said as he stormed off.

Adam went to the police station and told Carter what had just happened. Carter looked so distressed at Adam. With a little sigh he said, "Man. I told you she was letting this job go to her head."

Adam threw out some obscenities about what he thought of Candy, and Carter agreed.

Back at city hall Candy gave the keys to Denise and asked her to take care of canceling Adams city credit card.

Carter was tickled to death about this latest chain of events. After Adam left his office in a furry, Carter smiled to himself and thought 'job well done'.

Chapter 20

Over the next couple of months Carter played the role of best friend to Candy and Denise. He pretended to just hate what had happened with Adam. "You know Candy, this whole thing was wrong. The council only put you in the position of city manager to get rid of Adam. They didn't want to be the bad guys. They made you do it, then let Adam think it was all you're doing."

Candy had been thinking the same thing. Carter just planted it in her head as reality. "I think they did too."

Jobs were hard to find. Especially if you had the qualifications that Adam had. Every place he applied for a job, he had higher credentials than the people he would be under, so it was just impossible for him to find a job. He called Candy one night at home.

"Candy, I'm so sorry for what happened. The last couple of months I was working for the city I had a really bad attitude. I'm sorry for that, and I'd really like to come back to work. Do you think they will let me?"

Candy was so glad that Adam had called her. She liked Adam and hoped he could see through the city councils motives in making her city manager.

"I'll talk to them Adam. I just don't know what to expect from them."

Candy did talk to the city council. She told them what Adam said. "I think he really hates what happened. I'm sure if you let him come back you will see a change."

In the meantime, Adam called each of the city council members to plead his case. The only one who wouldn't talk to him was Larry.

They called a special city council meeting. Adam was there, and he told them how sorry he was for his behavior. The city council then went into executive session so no one would know what they each said. When they came out of the executive session they voted on whether to hire Adam back. The vote was "all in favor". Adam came back to work the next day.

Within days Carter was once again trying to poison Adam against Candy and Denise. There were two other part time workers in the office now. Carter was working on them as well. Every time Candy was out of the office, Carter would jump at the chance to work on manipulating the other workers. He had even made some attempts with Denise. He just had to get rid of Candy next. The rest would be easy. So he thought.

Chapter 21

Candy had become very well known throughout the state for her skills and knowledge for Municipal Government. She was asked to be a moderator at the International City Clerk conference in Whistler British Columbia Canada.

"Mrs. Patterson, this is Sharon Wheeler. I'm the conference planner for the International City Clerks Association. We were wondering if you would consider being a moderator for this year's conference in Canada."

"I would be very honored to be a moderator. What would you like for me to do?"

"We will be sending you a packet with all of the information on the speakers that you will be introducing. There will be bios included. When you get to the conference, tell the person at the registration desk who you are, and she will direct you to meet with me."

"Thank you so much for asking me. I'll see you at the conference."

After Candy ended her conversation with Sharon, she called Larry and told him. She was really excited, and honored to have been chosen.

Larry told her to put it on the agenda for the next council meeting. He said the city would pay for all of Candy's expenses for the trip to Canada.

This would be a chance of a lifetime. Candy had never been to Canada.

"Pat, will you go with me. I really don't want to go by myself. There will be other people from Oklahoma at the conference, but I'd rather spend my free time with you."

"Sure, I'll go with you."

The city council approved the trip. One of the council members said, "When you go on this trip, you are not to pay for one thing while you are there. Not even a pack of gum. The city is paying ALL of your expenses."

Now Candy had to make travel plans. She checked all the airlines to see what would be the best deal. She could book plane tickets for her and Pat together and get a bigger discount. To make things simpler, she gave the airline her city credit card information for both tickets.

"Hey Denise, I booked me and Pat's plane tickets and charged them on the city credit card. Here's a check from my personal checking account for Pat's ticket. I made it out to VISA. Just send this in with the credit card bill, and pay the rest with a city check."

"Okay. I'll just attach it to the purchase order for the plane tickets, and then I'll mail it with the city's check."

"Thanks."

Before she knew it, it was time to leave for Canada.

Pat and Candy left early that morning. When they got to Vancouver they rented a car and drove the rest of the way to Whistler.

It was about a 45 minute drive. It was amazing. It was just beautiful. It was early May. There was snow in places, but the trees were all in colorful bloom. There were water falls, mountains, and lakes that would just take your breath away.

Whistler Village was just that. A Village. There were very few cars. The ones that were there stayed parked most of the time. Everyone walked to get to where they were going. Most of the little café's had outside eating areas. There were outside heaters to keep you warm while you ate. There was a ski lift that seemed to go up to the heavens. Candy thought she could sit on a bench on the sidewalk and look at the beauty of this

After All is Said and Done....More is Said Than Done

place forever.

The conference was so educational and informative. Each morning Candy would get up, get dressed like she was going off to school, and walk over to the conference building. She would be in training sessions throughout the morning, and then Pat would meet her out front for lunch. They would walk somewhere for lunch, then Candy would go back for more sessions. The training was so much more than anything Candy had ever attended before.

At the end of the day, Candy would walk back to her hotel where she would meet Pat. They would walk somewhere for dinner.

Several nights were preplanned by the conference coordinator. They had all kinds of activities for them to enjoy. One night they went on a ride in a gondola up to the top of the mountain. Once they reached the top of the mountain, there was a beautiful lodge. All of the conference attendees were taken on a snow shoeing walk. The snow shoes looked like tennis rackets strapped to their feet.

After they returned to the lodge, the conference committee had a dinner and live music for them.

Candy had to do her introductions for speakers on the second day of the conference. She practiced and memorized everything on the bio about each of the speakers. She didn't want to look like a 'hick from Oklahoma' in front of all those people. She was determined to make Oklahoma proud that she was their representative.

Before she knew it, it was time to go back to Oklahoma. After she returned, she wrote an appreciation letter to the city council for giving her such a wonderful opportunity. She knew she would always cherish this experience.

She didn't know this would be the last good experience she would have while working for the Town of Hereford.

Chapter 22

It was time for another city council election and this time it got really nasty. This was the first time Candy had seen this happen in the Town of Hereford. Usually council members never even drew an opponent. This time Larry had a run for his money. And another council member, John Mannford, did as well. Both of them had opponents. John was a quiet man who really didn't want to be on the city council anyway. Larry was another story. Larry liked telling people that he was the Mayor.

Things weren't going right for Carter. He was beginning to get agitated and nervous, and he had a plan. He called Candy. "Candy, I just don't know what we're gonna do if we get new council members and they want all new people in here. We just have to come up with a plan. I've heard that people want to get rid of you, and we can't let this happen."

Candy was a little surprised. She knew there were a few people that she had run ins with over late water bills, and court fines, but all in all, she thought she was liked by most of the people. Now she was thinking maybe she was wrong.

"I don't know Carter. If people really want me out of here, maybe I need to start thinking about leaving."

Carter said he had been trying to figure out a plan to make sure Candy and Carter would still have a job after the election.

After a little more discussion Candy said, "Hey I know, let's get your friend at the newspaper to run. What's her name---- uhh--- Mary!" Candy was just kidding when she said it. Carter told stories all the time about what an idiot Mary was. Candy asked him one day if she knew that he talked about her like that, and he said "No. And if I wanted her to know I'd tell her."

After All is Said and Done....More is Said Than Done

Carter told Candy that he knew Mary would support Larry. Carter was getting pretty excited about this. He said, "We can work to get Mary in, and Larry re-elected, and we know John is for us. We'll have three on our side and that's all it takes."

This was working out just perfect for Carter. He could get Mary to do anything he wanted.

"You know I'll have to tell her everything to do and say if she gets elected. She won't have a clue as to what to do." Carter laughed.

Candy said, "You know, this might work. Mary likes us. Tell her that I'll help her!"

"She'll have to have help Candy. You'd really do that?"

"Sure, I'll help her every step of the way. I already do it for all the other city council members. I meet with Larry before every meeting to give him a briefing on what each of the agenda items are."

"You know, your right Candy, this just might work. I'll call her right now."

Hallelujah, Carter thought. Mary will be my puppet.

And indeed she was. Mary ran for city council with Carter right by her side doing all the campaign speeches for her. All she had to do was shake hands and kiss the babies. The people loved Carter, so she was a shoe in.

Larry on the other hand was a challenge. People didn't really like Larry. They said he had lied to them over the years, and the only reason he was still on the city council was because nobody else ran against him. Most of the city employees campaigned for Larry. They were making all kinds of excuses for him.

Chapter 23

On the agenda for the city council meeting, Larry put, "Discussion of personnel, Council may go into executive session."

On the night of the meeting, Council member Lloyd Hanna made a motion to go into executive session.

Council member Jack Morton said, "Guys, I don't think we can do that, because the agenda item isn't worded right. It has to be specific according to state law."

Lloyd rolled his eyes at Jack. None of the council members liked Jack. He wasn't the sharpest pencil in the rack.

Jack looked at Lloyd and shouted, "Do you not think that what I'm telling you is right!"

Lloyd just wasn't in the mood to fight with Jack tonight. Lloyd looked at Larry and said "Mr. Mayor, I make a motion that we table this item until the next meeting."

Everyone voted in favor except Jack who voted "no". Jack looked like his feelings were so hurt. He looked over at Candy and said, "Candy, I want it noted in the minutes that I voted no!"

Candy nodded her head and said "okay Jack."

***

Jack came into city hall the next day. Candy was sitting in her office. She heard Jack talking to Adam. Candy had a private office now. The door to her office connected to the lobby.

Jack said, "I felt ambushed by Larry at the council meeting last night. He shot me in the back with an arrow that I'm still trying to get out, and I'm not gonna put up with it! You know who to vote for on election day don't you?"

Candy couldn't hear Adams reply. Ben, Adam's side-kick, walked into Candy's office and sat down. Then Candy heard Jack say, "Not Larry!"

Candy looked at Ben and said "What did he just say?" and Ben replied, "I don't know. Something about Larry ambushing him. I came in here cause I didn't want to hear what he was saying."

Jack walked into Candy's office and asked Candy, "Are you and Ben having a private conversation?" Ben said "No, I was just waiting for Adam." Then Ben left the office.

Jack sat down in the chair in front of Candy's desk. Then in a really irritated tone, he said, "I felt like I was ambushed by Larry at the council meeting last night. I didn't want to go into executive session because when I got to city hall for the meeting, I asked Larry why personnel was on the agenda, and he wouldn't give me an answer."

Candy never had cared much for Jack, and Jack didn't like her either. He thought she had way to much control.

When Jack was first elected to the city council, Candy tried to help him understand that there are things that you just can't do, but that didn't work out very well. Jack would argue with a fence post, and council meetings were the worst. Especially if Jack had an audience. He walked out of several council meetings, just to make a statement.

Jack told Candy that he asked Larry if that agenda item was to talk about Shawn, and Larry told him "yes".

There was an employee, Shawn Martin, who was the code enforcement officer. Jack wanted to do all kinds of favors for Shawn. Favors that couldn't be done. Candy didn't understand why Jack was so partial to Shawn, but he was. He wanted to give him a higher rate of pay than the pay scale, he wanted to give him bonuses, and the list went on and on.

Jack started in on Candy again. "Why can't we do more for Shawn?" Candy explained it all to Jack again, for about the fourth time. Jack seemed so surprised. Like he had never heard these explanations before. He said, "Well, does Shawn know why I can't get these things for him?" Candy told him that she had talked to Shawn about it.

After Jack left Candy's office he went straight to the police station to talk to Carter. "Carter, I just don't understand why Candy won't help me get more for Shawn. Do you understand why?" Carter said, "Well, yes Jack, I do." Then Carter went over it again with Jack. Jack said, "I wonder why Candy never told me that."

***

Three days later Jack paid Candy another visit. He asked Candy if she had a copy of the personnel policy. She told him that she did. Jack then said, "You know it's in the personnel policy in section 16 dash 1 number 11, that employees can't campaign". Candy just couldn't believe this. She knew this was because she and the other employees were campaigning for Larry. Jack looked sternly at Candy and said, "I'd hate for anyone to lose their job over it. The employees could get fired for campaigning. You might want to make a copy of that section of the personnel policy and give it to all of the employees." Candy told him that she would make sure all of the employees got a copy. After all, Jack was one of her bosses. Candy made copies of it, and put one in each of the employee mailboxes in city hall.

Later that day, Carter came in to get his mail. He wanted to know why a page from the personnel policy was in his mailbox. Candy told him about the conversation that she had earlier with Jack. Carter called Jack.

"Hey Jack, I got this paper in my mailbox and I want to

After All is Said and Done....More is Said Than Done

know what your take on it is, because you do understand that this means we can't campaign on duty or in City Hall, but the town can't prevent us from exercising our constitutional rights."

After Carter got off the phone he told Candy that he felt threatened by Jack. He said Jack told him that he would hate to see someone lose their job over this. Then Carter said, "I'm taking those papers out of the employee's mail boxes."

***

Things were just so crazy at work. With the election coming up, there was so much arguing, and people trying to win people to their side. Candy was a nervous wreck. She and Denise both were physically drained.

It had been two days since Candy's last encounter with Jack. When she woke up to get ready to go to work that morning she was so sick she couldn't hold her head up. Every time she moved she felt like she was going to throw up. She called Denise and told her that she wasn't going to be there.

When Candy returned to work the next day, Denise told her that Jack came into City hall the day before, just trying to upset everyone. She said that Carter and Jack had words. She said that Jack said, "Who took the copies of the personnel policy out of the mailboxes?" Fact was, Carter had told Shawn about taking the copies out of the mail boxes, and Shawn high-tailed it over to Jack's house to tell him. Denise said that when Jack asked about the copies being removed from the mailboxes, she didn't answer. She said that Jack just went on and on about campaigning being against policy.

Denise told Candy that before Jack left city hall he filled out a request to put an item on the agenda for the next city council meeting. The request said, "Do a seven year employment contract with Carter". Denise told Candy that she laid the paper on Candy's desk.

Candy read the paper. "What is this all about? I just can't figure that guy out."

Denise said, "I have no idea. Just something to get under Carter's skin I guess."

Candy called the City Attorney, but she already knew the answer. He told her the town couldn't do a seven year contract with Carter, or anyone else for that matter. Since council members are only elected for four year terms, they can't make obligations for a council member who may take their place.

Candy wrote "CAN'T DO" on the paper that Jack had filled out. Then she put it in Jack's mail box. Jack came in city hall later that day to check his mail. He looked at Candy's note and said, "Didn't think we could do that" then walked out.

A few minutes later, Carter called Candy and said that Jack was following him around town, and he wasn't going to talk to him without a witness. Carter said, "I'm coming to your office Candy."

Carter went to city hall and Jack followed. They both walked into Candy's office. Jack handed the note Candy had written "CAN'T DO" on, to Carter.

Carter wadded the paper up and threw it into Candy's trash can by her desk. Then he said, "Jack why are you causing so much trouble. It's no wonder Lloyd wants to jerk your hat down around your throat."

Jack started to walk out, and then he turned back to Carter and said, "You just take things wrong."

Carter was furious. He shouted, "What about the deal with the campaigning, and employees losing their jobs!"

Jack turned to Candy and said, "Did you see anything wrong with that?"

Candy was getting pretty agitated by this point. She said,

After All is Said and Done....More is Said Than Done

"Yes, I did Jack. I have a right to sit on my couch at nine o'clock at night, and call every single person in the town, and ask them to vote for Larry if I want to. I know I can't stand out there in the lobby and campaign for him, but what I do after hours is my business. We all know that the reason you're doing this is because you don't like Larry."

Carter said, "Let's just get it all out in the open here Jack. You want Shawn to be the Chief of Police, and you want to be the city manager!"

Jack stammered a little then said, "No I don't want to be city manager.... but, okay, I would make some changes if I could. I would have Candy working on grants. And I want to be Mayor!"

Well, there it was. Jack wanted to be Mayor, but he knew that as long as Larry was around that wouldn't happen.

Carter said, "What you really want is this office right here!"

Jack shook his head no. "I really do want to be Mayor, and I wouldn't mind having a desk, and a phone, so I could make some calls." Jack then turned to leave. As he was going out the door he looked at Carter and said, "Carter, I've always supported you. Candy, thank you."

Candy was wonder who in the world Jack was wanting to call. She supposed it was just the status of being Mayor, having a desk and phone. How weird.

Carter and Candy talked to the City Attorney about everything that had been happening. The City Attorney told them that he was going to talk to all of the City Council members and tell them that a hostile environment was being created, and if they didn't get control of the situation things could get terribly out of hand.

The next day Candy was sick and stayed home from work again.

Chapter 24

Thank Goodness the election was over. Larry and Mary won. John lost to Mark Jackson. Lloyd and Jack didn't have to run this time so they were still on board.

Mark was a short chubby guy in his 30's. He had shoulder length black hair that he slicked back with gel, or oil, or something. He had a black mustache to match. He was the most hyper guy Candy had ever met. It was really hard to hold a conversation with him. His mind was wondering all the time. Carter said "He acts like a kid on Ritalin". Candy said, "No, he acts like a kid who needs Ritalin."

This was going to be an interesting four years.

After the election, Carter started playing the employees against each other again. There were employee grievances, which led to a council meeting and executive session.

Carter sat in on the executive session. He told the city council that he thought everyone was plotting against him. He told them that he started imagining things which led to him acting like he did. He told them that he was going to see a doctor, and a counselor, because he was really his worst enemy.

Lloyd told Candy and Denise to let him know if Carter started causing trouble again. "I think everything is going to work itself out now girls. Things are going to be okay."

Apparently the counseling sessions for Carter weren't working. He told Candy that the reason for all of the problems with the employees was because of Denise. "We didn't have all this drama until Denise started working here. And another thing, Adam and Josh can't be trusted. I'm trying to stay in good with those two so they will tell me stuff that I can pass on to you. Be careful what you say to them Candy."

One evening Carter called Denise at home. When she saw who it was on the caller ID she didn't answer. Carter called Denise several more times, but she didn't answer. Denise called Candy. In a frustrated tone Denise said, "Candy, Carter keeps calling me. I haven't answered the phone though."

Candy sighed. "Okay, I'll call Lloyd and tell him. I'll call you back and let you know what he says."

Candy called Lloyd and told him what Denise had said. Lloyd was really aggravated at Carter. "I don't know what's wrong with that guy. I've tried giving him hints to stop his trouble making but apparently it didn't work. I'll take care of it."

Candy called Denise back to let her know what Lloyd had said. She said Carter had called her three times since she had talked to her.

The next morning Lloyd had a talk with Carter. He was pretty harsh with him. Later in the afternoon Mary called Denise. "I think it's just terrible the way you are treating Carter. He is so hurt."

Denise didn't know what to say to Mary. She just sat there and listened to Mary berate her.

About a week later Carter started calling city hall again. Candy and Denise were both very careful about what they said to him. They wanted to be able to work with him without all the nonsense. During the phone calls, Carter kept telling Candy and Denise to watch out for Adam and Ben. He said "I have a code name for them. Let's call them Mutt and Jeff, that way if they hear us talking they won't know we are talking about them." Candy and Denise just handled things the best they could.

During one of Carter's crazy calls, he told Candy, "Did you

know that Lloyd wants to be the Mayor? He said he needs to take control of everything. I have to make sure that don't happen. He's been after me, and I have to stop him."

Several months of Carter's obsession to "survive" as he would say, went on. He was really getting annoyed with Mary now. "I have to tell her everything to do and say. The other day I told her what to do about getting a nutrition program started for senior citizens, and she argued with me about it. I've been dealing with this ever since the election!"

Candy had had enough. In April 2005 Candy submitted her resignation as city manager.

"I respectfully request that I be removed from my duties as City Manager. However, I will continue to serve in the capacity of my other job duties as City Clerk/Treasurer.

I have given this many hours of consideration and feel that it would be in the best interest of the Town and myself.

Each Department has a supervisor who is fully capable of continuing daily operations without any disruptions due to this change.

I do feel that my salary should be adjusted accordingly, since I did get a raise when I assumed the position of City Manager. With your approval, I will make the adjustment with the April payroll.

My goal has always been to do the best that I could do for the Town, and to obtain all the knowledge and education available to perform my job. I appreciate all that you have done for me, and will continue to strive for improvement.

Sincerely,
Candy Patterson

Chapter 25

The parents of a 16 year old boy sat in the Police station listening to Carter lecture their son about staying out of trouble. Carter wasn't a good police officer, so he tried to be a good councilor. He was the 'Big Brother' for Hereford.

The town now had four police officers. Carter had gotten so involved in his counseling practices that it was taking up all of his time. He was rarely seen out working the streets, but he could almost always be found at the police station with the door locked.

Everyone knew that Candy was a Christian and attended a little country church. She talked about it often. Carter couldn't wait to tell her that he had joined a church. Everyone would be so impressed. His thoughts were spinning.

Just a couple of weeks after Carter announced to everyone that he was attending church, he started trying to get everyone to come to church with him. Even Candy. Oh, this church was better than any place he had ever been.

Candy was glad that Carter was in church, but she hoped it was for the right reasons. He just seemed so pushy about getting people to leave the churches they already attended.

Sitting at her desk working, Denise looked over at Candy and said, "What do you think about this deal with Carter and church?"

Candy said, "I don't know but he sure is fired up about it."

"Yes he is. Did he tell you his latest? He told a kid the other day that if he would show up in 'HIS' (emphasis on the his) church for the next four Sundays, that he would void a ticket that one of the other officers had written to him for speeding."

"YOU MUST BE KIDDING!"

"No I'm not."

That was just the beginning. Every few days Candy would get a complaint that Carter had made a deal with someone to fix a ticket if they showed up at his church. One of the street workers told Candy that Carter tried to make a deal with his cousin, but his cousin told Carter that he attended his own church. Carter told him "No deal" unless he attended his church. The street workers cousin said he would just pay the ticket.

Carter was having Denise to hold tickets, then after a few weeks, sometimes he would say, "Go ahead and put that one on the docket" or "Void that one. " It had gotten so bad that Denise just had to speak to Candy about the ticket fixing. Denise had done some checking and found out that it was illegal for Carter to void other officer's tickets, or even his own if they had been turned in to the Court Clerk. All of the tickets that Carter had told Denise to void were tickets written by the other guys in the police department. Carter rarely wrote a ticket since he spent most of his time in the police station.

Denise sat down by Candy's desk and said, "We have a little problem that I need to talk to you about."

Candy looked up at Denise. "Okay, what's wrong Denise?"

"I had to void four more tickets today. Sometimes Carter calls me and says 'Do you have a ticket on so-and-so? I need you to hold onto that for a few days.' Then if the kid goes to church, or washes Carter's car, or whatever it is Carter decides for him to do, he calls me and tells me to void the ticket. And none of the tickets are written by Carter. They are all written by the other guys."

Candy suspected things were getting out of hand, but she was hoping that Carter would get over his latest craze before she had to deal with it. "I'll talk to him right away Denise.

Thanks for letting me know."

Candy called Carter. "I just thought you should know that an officer in a little town outside of Oklahoma City is being investigated by OSBI for this very same thing. Don't get yourself caught up in something you can't get out of Carter."

"I'm just trying to help these kids and their parents. If those tickets go before the Judge, and to the State, it's just going to cost the parents a lot of money, and the kid hasn't learned anything."

"Maybe so Carter, but that's not legal."

When Carter hung up the phone he was furious. Denise would pay for this.

Chapter 26

Municipal Court was held the second Tuesday of every month at 9 A.M. Judge Bailey usually got to city hall a little early and would sit and visit with Candy. They had always had a very good working relationship. Candy had a lot of respect for Judge Bailey.

Carter was waiting outside for Judge Bailey to arrive. He had to talk to the Judge before Candy did. Carter was so paranoid. He just knew that Candy had already called OSBI on him, and an investigation was under way. His mind imagined all kinds of things that weren't true.

Carter nervously approached Judge Bailey as the Judge was getting out of his car. "Mornin Judge."

"Morning Carter. You need something."

"I have a little problem I need to talk to you about if you have a minute."

"Okay. What's going on?"

"Well Judge, Candy is trying to get me into trouble for voiding a couple of tickets. You know those guys who work for me are green, and I'm always having to get them out of messes."

The Judge didn't say a word. Carter continued. He told the Judge about how stupid the guys were who worked under him, and that they were always writing tickets, then coming to him and asking his advice. "Sometimes I tell them that they really should have just had a heart to heart talk with the person they wrote the ticket to. I don't' want the public to think they can get out of a ticket if one of my guys writes them, so instead of just throwing the ticket out, I make them do some community service or something."

After All is Said and Done....More is Said Than Done

The Judge listened to Carter as he rambled trying to defend his actions. Judge Bailey looked seriously at Carter and said, "Don't do that anymore Carter. The only one who has the authority to sentence community service is me, and once those tickets are turned in to the Court Clerk, they are no longer the officers. You can't legally void a ticket once it has been turned in to the Court Clerk."

Carter started trying to defend himself again, and Judge Bailey raised his hand as if telling Carter that was enough, and said, "Just don't do it anymore." Judge Bailey walked away.

Carter wasn't sure how that conversation just went, but he hoped the Judge would tell Candy and Denise to back off.

As soon as court was over that day, Carter left the court room. Usually he would hang around and visit, but not today. After Carter left, Candy went back to the court room to talk to the Judge. Denise was already telling him about what Carter had been doing. The Judge told Candy and Denise that Carter had talked to him a little bit before court, but he didn't know it was as bad as it was. He told them that Carter didn't tell him all of it. Judge Bailey said, "Let's just hope that he don't do it anymore."

But Carter did continue to sentence people to community service. He wasn't going to let anyone tell him how to run his police department. The only difference was, instead of letting the other officers turn in their tickets to Denise, they had to turn them in to Carter. Then Carter would hold them, or void them, or whatever he wanted, as long as he wanted. That way Denise wouldn't know if he voided the ticket, or the officer who wrote the ticket voided it. He was so proud of himself for thinking of that one. "You will pay for this Denise", Carter smugly said to himself.

Chapter 27

Denise worked so hard. She was good at her job, but she was just too close to Candy. Carter wanted her gone. He thought he may be able to kill two birds with one stone. He may be able to turn Candy and Denise against each other before this was over with, but for now he had a little something in store for Denise.

Carter told a contractor, Zack Gibson, who had bid on a project for the town, that Denise had given out their bid information to another contractor who was her friend. Carter told Zach that Denise did it so her friend could bid less than Zack on the job. This opened a huge can of worms. Zach filed a complaint with the city council, and they were ready to fire Denise over it. Denise was so upset. She talked to Larry and told him that she didn't give out any sealed bid information. She cried every time she tried to talk to Candy about it. Candy was getting madder by the minute, and she had finally had her fill.

Once again, the city council called a special meeting. Candy was sitting in her office when everyone started gathering for the meeting. Zach Gibson was there, along with people in town who heard there was going to be trouble, and just wanted to be there for the show.

After all the council members were seated in their designated chairs at the long meeting table, Larry said, "I'll go get Candy." He walked over to Candy's desk and said, "Babe, you ready." She looked up at Larry and said, "No Larry, I'm not. I'm just not going to do this." She got her purse, turned off her desk light, and walked out the door.

Later that night Denise called Candy and said. "What happened to you? I was worried about you. Larry came back there and said you weren't feeling well, and you left. He asked me to take the minutes of the meeting."

Candy was still so mad. "I just couldn't do it Denise. It makes me so mad that the City Council believes Carter. I'm not sure if I'll ever come back."

Denise told Candy that the city council asked her if she did what Carter said. And she once again told them that she didn't. Carter told them that he was just saying what someone else had told him. He didn't actually know if Denise did it or not. He explained that he was just trying to keep everyone out of trouble.

Candy didn't go to work for three more days. She really didn't think she would go back to work, but Pat told her that she should at least go back until everything was cleared up. So finally on the fourth day she went into work. When Carter saw that she was back, he called Mary and told her to call another special meeting so they could reprimand Candy.

"Mary, you can't fire her because she's never had anything disciplinary in her file, but this is a start. You can give her a written warning. Tell her she only gets one. One more and she's out the door."

Mary, being Carter's puppet, was all over it. A special meeting was called for that afternoon. The only thing on the agenda was '*disciplinary action for city clerk*'. Candy was ready for them. She told Denise, "They don't want to do this. I'm not going to cry, but someone might before this is over."

After the meeting was called to order, the council decided to go into executive session and asked Candy to come in with them. Once they were all seated, Mary looked at Candy and said, "Candy we need to get some things straight." And that's when Candy let them know what she thought.

She told Mary that Carter talks about her like she's an idiot.

Carla Reed

That they all have listened to Carter's lies and believed him. She told them that she thought they were smart enough to think on their own, but apparently not, because they had all fallen under his manipulation. They all just sat there in silence while Candy vented. She told them that anything discussed in executive session was supposed to be kept confidential, but Mary tells Carter everything they discuss. She told them that Carter tells everyone that he has to lead Mary around and tell her everything to say and do. She told Mary that the phone call to chew Denise out because she had hurt Carter's feelings was over the top. She told them that the accusations about Denise were ridiculous. Candy felt like she was playing out the song, *The day my momma socked it to the Harper Valley PTA.*

Mary was in tears by the time Candy finished. They all looked a little like they had been slapped. One of the council members said, "I told you all. And for you Mary, Carter has made sure that you have no creditably as a council member. I say let's dismiss this meeting and go home." Candy walked out of the executive session feeling pretty relieved about what she had just done. Now maybe things could get back to normal around here.

Candy told Denise that everything was resolved. "They know you didn't do it Denise. Just hang in there. Let's just try to come to work, do our job, and hope that everyone leaves us alone. I hate the drama that goes on around here, and we know who causes it."

Carter wasn't very pleased that Mary wasn't able to do better than she did in the meeting. He knew he couldn't count on her if she got out there on a limb by herself. If only they wouldn't have gone behind closed doors he could have helped her out. Now he had to come up with another plan just because Mary is as stupid as he'd told everyone she was.

Chapter 28

Hereford had a volunteer fire department. It was an all-male organization. The guys were very chauvinistic. They said, "There ain't no woman who can do what we do. This here is man's work."

Once you were accepted into the Volunteer Fire Fighter Brotherhood, you were immediately transformed into a dedicated, important part of society. Most of the guys drove red pickup trucks with stickers all over them representing their fire fighter status. Any time of the day, you might see a couple of the guys in town wearing their 'Fire Fighter' T-shirts. Some of the guys had every piece of their apparel monogrammed with their name on one side, and 'Fire Fighter' on the other.

The Hereford Police Department had an old vehicle that they weren't using any more. They decided to let the fire department use it to run around in since they were using their own personal vehicles to go to training in Oklahoma City, and to go pick up parts and supplies, or just whatever. They immediately took the old car and had it outfitted with stickers and emblems. Just to make it look really official, they put 'Fire Chief' in big letters across both sides of the vehicle.

It didn't take long for complaints to start pouring in to Candy about the misuse of the vehicle.

The fire chief was an unemployed guy by the name of Roger. Roger was your typical redneck. Loved to hunt coons (that's a whole other story), drink beer, and play poker. He had 'Fire Chief tattooed on the lower part of his arm so it could be easily seen. He thought since he was the fire chief, the car was his to use whenever, and however he chose. He said he kept the car parked in his driveway so he would have quick access to fires, when in fact he drove it for his own personal use. The big problem with that was that the town of Hereford was paying for all the gas.

That wasn't the only misuse of city funds that Roger was involved in. The fire department had a fireworks stand every year, and the money they made off of it was used for other fire department events. They used it for a big Christmas party. They had a party in the summer, and they used the money to help families with emergencies. One day Roger had an emergency.

Denise called Roger and told him that he was three months behind on his water bill. "Roger, I've covered for you as long as I can. You're going to have to pay this today. If Candy, or the City Council, finds out that I've let you go this long, I could be in trouble. If I don't get payment on this by two o'clock I'm going to have to send the guys out to shut your water off."

Roger said, "I don't have any money."

"Well, I don't know what to tell you. If you can't come up with the money we'll have to shut your water off."

Then Roger said, "Hey wait. I think I can pay it. I have to open the fireworks stand at ten o'clock. I'll be over after that."

"Okay Roger. I'm really sorry."

Denise walked into Candy's office and told her about what Roger had said. Candy looked up at Denise and said, "Okay - He don't have any money - But after he opens the fireworks stand, he'll have money. So don't that sound to you like he's using money from the fireworks stand to pay his water bill?"

Denise said, "That's what it sounds like."

Roger came into city hall at 10:15 A.M. and paid his water bill in full.

Candy knew she was going to have to talk to the City

After All is Said and Done....More is Said Than Done

Council about Roger. He had started going to the truck stop, filling the car with gas, and charging it to the city almost every day. It was quite obvious that he was driving the car for his personal use.

Candy spoke to Larry about the misuse of the vehicle, and he said he would ask Carter to do an investigation. Candy said, "Why don't you just talk to Roger and tell him not to do that anymore? You and I both know it's illegal."

Larry said, "Let's just let Carter handle it, okay."

Candy knew why Larry didn't want to confront Roger. That's the way he always handled problems. Let someone else do it. If she had still been City Manager, Larry would have told her to talk to Roger.

A few days later Carter called Candy and told her that Roger was no longer on the fire department. "I've been getting a lot of complaints about him using that car. He's even been seen in Tulsa at the movies in it. I asked him about it, and he denied it. I told him that I could prove it. I told him about the gas tickets, and he still denied it. Then I told him that if he didn't resign from the fire department I was going to file charges on him, so he resigned." Carter never mentioned that Larry had told him to talk to Roger.

Candy had expected this. "So who's going to be the Chief now?"

"I don't know. The fire fighters are having a meeting on Tuesday. They'll pick someone then."

Chapter 29

The next two years were miserable for Denise and Candy. They became very distant with all of the employees. They only associated with each other. They tried to just keep business as business with everyone else.

Denise just couldn't get over what Carter and the City Council had put her through. She knew it was just a matter of time before Carter struck again.

Denise started applying for jobs, and with her skills and personality, it didn't take her long to find something. She really hated to leave Candy. She knew Carter was going to make her life miserable. And what a shame that was. Candy was so good at her job, and people really liked her. The people of Hereford knew how hard she worked for them. Candy had worked for the Town of Hereford for 18 years now.

There was a woman working part time in the office who wanted to step into Denise's position. Her name was Sara James. Sara seemed like a nice enough person. She certainly wasn't Marla or Denise, but Candy told the City Council that she wouldn't have any trouble working with her. Sara seemed to have a lot of self-confidence, although Candy wasn't sure why. She really wasn't qualified to do Denise's job. She dropped out of high school in the 10th grade, and her grammar was just terrible. She often used the words, "I done it" and "there aint no". She was on the heavy side, although she was always on a new diet. She had a tight curly perm, and she was proud to tell people that she "loved those Ogleve home perms". About the only thing she had going for her was that the people in Hereford seemed to like her. She was always friendly and helpful to the customers. Sara was a prime candidate for

After All is Said and Done....More is Said Than Done

Carter to manipulate. He had already spent some time getting to know Sara, and he knew she could be influenced easily.

Sara hadn't been working for the town of Hereford very long when Denise gave her two week notice, but she was learning how to do the water bills. The City Council decided to give her a try in Denise's position, so Denise started training her. Candy took back all the court clerk duties, and about half of the other things that Denise did. Candy just hoped that with time Sara would be able to pick up some of the slack.

Poor Sara, she didn't have any idea how to get untangled from Carter's web. Heck, she didn't even know she was in his web. One day after Denise had resigned, Sara told Candy that Denise had warned her about Carter. Sara said, "I know he's evil. I'm not gonna listen to him, but do you know what he told me."

Candy said, "No, what's that Sara?"

Sara was standing by Candy's desk with her hands on her hips. She spoke in her smartest hillbilly voice. "He came over to my desk one day and was whisperin like he had a big secret. He says, you know you could be runnin this place one of these days. All you have to do is work real hard and learn ever thang. He even said he'd help me onest you was gone."

Candy didn't doubt for one minute that Carter had said those things. Candy started to laugh and said, "Really?"

Sara said, "Yep, he said that. And I told him I don't wont to run this place."

Candy just didn't know what else to say to Sara. She kind of felt sorry for her because she knew that Carter would be able to convince her of anything. Sara on the other hand, was thinking the whole time she was talking to Candy that she was going to be behind Candy's desk soon. Sara sure hoped Carter was right about what he had told her. She never dreamed she could land a deal like this.

Chapter 30

The employees, and council members, were really taking a toll on Candy. More than she even realized. It was so stressful dealing with the constant turmoil, but on the other hand, Candy loved the work she did. She poured herself into her work. She lived and breathed 'Hereford'. It was past time to have a life outside of work.

The sign out front read '*Lake Eufaula Country Kitchen - Family owned and operated*'. Candy's brother James, and his wife Lisa, had opened a restaurant on the lake. It was known for the best country cookin' around.

They opened on Memorial weekend. What a bad idea! The first big weekend of the summer, with hundreds of hungry campers. Family operated was exactly right. Everyone came to help. Candy, Natalee, Cale, Abby, Annie, Seth, Maggie ..... They were all there.

By the end of the weekend, they were so exhausted, but they were pretty excited that James had such a good business. He was already figuring out what he would do differently to make things go better for the next weekend. Over the following week things would be slower. He could work out all the kinks and be ready when the weekend came.

Candy and Pat started spending weekends at the lake again, and Candy helped out some at the restaurant on Saturday. She didn't work on Sunday. She was always in church on Sunday.

Candy didn't know one thing about restaurant work, but she was learning. James was the cook, and a very good cook at that. Lisa took care of the business end of things. Candy's sister Annie washed dishes and kept the buffet replenished. Natalee waited tables, and Candy mostly just cleaned, helped her sister Natalee out some, and visited with the customers. It was a nice break away from city hall.

Chapter 31

The old house had sat empty for seven years now. It was time to do something with it. Candy and Pat decided they would sell the house they were in, and buy Audrey and Herb's old house from Candy's brothers and sisters.

Candy and Pat's house sold quickly. They made a nice profit on it, so they had a good down payment for Candy's Mom and Dad's old place. They did a bank loan for the rest.

They would need a place to live until the new house was built so they bought a 40' trailer house to live in. It was nice enough, but it was crowded. They would be glad to get out of there.

The house was literally falling down. It sat on four acres of grown up, junked up land. Nothing had been done to it since Audrey and Herb passed away. It would take a lot of work, but Candy had always wanted to live there. When Candy was still in high school, she and Audrey were sitting at the kitchen table one night talking, and Audrey told Candy that if Herb passed away before her, she would sell the place. She said she couldn't live there without Herb.

"Oh Mom, I just don't see how you could just sell out. This was Grandpa's before it was yours and Great Grandpa's before that."

"I know, but I just couldn't stay here. I will probably move to the lake."

"If that happens, I'll buy it from you. I want to live here. I'm going to build me a new house here one of these days."

And so the time had come for Candy to tear down the old house and build her new home.

Dozers were brought in, and all the land cleared off. A few

trees were left, but nothing else.

The new house was just beautiful. They had rock work done on the outside, and a ten foot wrap around porch with white railing all the way around. Candy had steps going up to the front door built that were ten feet wide, with railing that matched the porch railing. There were big round columns at each corner of the steps.

Candy and Abby put down sod on the front lawn, and Pat seeded the other acreage. Candy knew her Mom and Dad would be so proud if they could see it.

People were talking all over town about how beautiful it was. Candy had several people come by just to take a look because they wanted a home that looked just like it. Candy even gave a piece of the rock to a lady so she could make sure her builder used the right one.

Candy thought this was where she would live until she died.

Chapter 32

Nothing was the same any more. Candy had been working for the town of Hereford for almost twenty years now. She still liked the work but she sure didn't like the people she worked with. Many sleepless nights, Candy lay awake thinking '*I should have quit working for the town of Hereford three years ago*'.

There were some good things going for Candy. Cale was an engineer now. He was married, and had a one year old baby girl that Candy adored. Abby was a successful Doctor. She lived in Oklahoma City with her best friend, a miniature schnauzer named Duchess. Although Candy didn't get to see Cale and Abby as often as she liked, they were still very close. Candy always told people that her kids were the best thing she ever did in her life.

They spoke to each other on the phone almost every day. Cale lived just twenty miles away, and Abby was just a couple of hours away.

Candy and Pat were still very much in love, and loved being together.

Denise had been gone for almost a year. There was fussing and fighting among the employees as usual. Carter stirred the pot daily. He would corner Adam and tell him lies about Candy and Sara. Then he would call Candy and tell her things about Adam and Sara. Then he would tell Sara things about Candy and Adam. And all the while, he told each one of them that they were one of his closest friends "and please don't tell anyone I told you this". Carter made sure he included the city council members in all of it too. Larry was the only city council member left that was on the council when Candy

After All is Said and Done....More is Said Than Done

started working for the Town of Hereford. Life at Hereford city hall was just terrible. Everyone hated each other. Candy dreaded going to work. She looked for every opportunity to be out of the office.

Cale's wife Laura, had decided to go to work, but they just hated to take the baby to day care. Laura's Mom could keep the baby two days a week, Laura's grandma could keep the baby two days, so that just left Wednesday. Candy wanted to stay home with that baby so badly.

It was decided. Candy called Larry with her plan. "I was wondering if I can start working 4 - 10 hour days for a while. Laura is going back to work and needs someone to keep the baby on Wednesdays. Wednesday is my slow day, and I can schedule any meetings on a different day."

"I don't see any reason why you can't do that. Sure."

Candy was pretty excited about it. She would much rather be home with the baby than at city hall.

Candy loved baby Elizabeth so much. She looked forward to Wednesday every week.

***

Tom Blocker was the newest on the board. Lloyd had just quit coming to council meetings. The state law says if you miss more than half of the council meetings in a four month period, you are automatically removed from the board. The city council appointed Tom to take Lloyd's place on the board, until the next city council election.

Tom had an auto repair shop. Oklahoma law says that if you are a council member, and own a business, the Town where you serve as a council member cannot do business with you. It would be a conflict of interest. This was another law that the city council chose to ignore.

The fire department took one of their trucks over to Tom's

shop and had some work done on it. When Candy saw the purchase order she called Larry and told him that the city could not legally pay the bill. "Larry, you guys know it's illegal to do business with Tom."

"Oh, it'll be okay. The name of his business don't have his name on it."

Tom's business was called *'The Shop'*.

Candy was so tired of trying to keep the city council out of trouble. "That don't matter. Everyone knows its Tom's business. You, Tom, and all the other council members could be in trouble if you approve that purchase order."

"I don't think anyone will find out. Just go ahead and pay it."

"Okay Larry. Whatever you say."

Larry must have mentioned something to Tom, because he started needing things on Wednesdays.

Candy still had a job to do, so she often went in to city hall at five or six o'clock on Wednesday morning and worked a couple of hours. Laura would drop the baby off at city hall on her way to work, and then Candy would take the baby and go home. Even with Candy being off on Wednesday, she was working about fifty to sixty hours a week. Candy worked a lot of hours that she didn't put on her time card. She took work home sometimes, but she really didn't want the council to know, because she was afraid they would make her start working on Wednesdays again.

There were a couple of times when Tom showed up at city hall and needed Candy to do something before she left. He acted like it really irritated him that Candy had the baby.

Then Tom started calling Candy at home on Wednesday. He needed her to come find something, or he needed her to write a letter for him. Candy always managed to get done

After All is Said and Done....More is Said Than Done

whatever Tom needed.

Candy sensed that Tom was getting back at her for talking to Larry about the repair bill, but at least there wasn't any more work done at *'The Shop'*.

Chapter 33

When Candy started working for the Town of Hereford, everything was done on paper. The town had a computer to do the water bills, but it didn't calculate the bills correctly about half the time. Candy had to go through the billing register every month and make corrections before the bills went out. That was a habit that Candy never got out of. Even with the new computer system, she went over that billing register with a fine tooth comb every month. She usually took it home with her and worked on it the night before bills were printed. Then she would take it back to city hall the next morning and give it to Sara so she could make corrections and print the water bills.

Most of the financial business for the town was done by Candy. Sara prepared the purchase orders, and then Candy would write the checks. Bank statements were balanced on the computer, and many of the bills were paid by electronic transfer. Times had really changed.

Candy did most of her personal banking online. She rarely paid a bill by sending a check in the mail. She paid her bills through the bank website, or by automatic draft.

Pat was semi-retired now. He had hung up his hat on chasing bad guys. Now he just did transporting of inmates. He traveled all over the country picking up people who had warrants for them. People would skip out, then end up getting picked up in other cities and states. When a record check was run on them, and there was an outstanding warrant in Oklahoma, Pat would go pick them up and bring them back.

A lot of times if Pat had to transport a juvenile or a female, Candy went with him. Pat had to make a trip to New Mexico to pick up a woman, and asked Candy if she wanted to ride along. They decided to leave on Friday morning, pick the woman up Saturday, then drive straight back.

On their way back home, they stopped at a convenience store to get gas and snacks. It was always Candy's job to go into the store and get snacks when they were on these trips. Candy paid the clerk for the drinks and chips. She laid her wallet on the counter so she could gather everything up. After a long day of riding she was pretty tired, and she walked right out of the store without her wallet. She didn't realize she didn't have her wallet until they were in Amarillo Texas.

As soon as they pulled into their driveway at home, Candy went into the house and called information to get the phone number for the store where she had left her wallet. She called the store, and the clerk told her they didn't have her wallet. Candy then called the credit card companies to cancel the cards she had in her wallet. "I have to go down to city hall Pat. I had a city credit card in my wallet, and I don't have the information here to cancel it. I'll be right back." Candy went to city hall and found the information she needed. She called the credit card company and canceled the card. She would have to deal with her lost checkbook first thing Monday morning.

Monday morning Candy told Sara what had happened. Sara just had a blank look on her face.

"I have to run over to the bank and talk to them about my check book Sara. I'll be right back."

When Candy spoke with the teller at the bank, she was told that she should close her checking account and open a new one "just in case". Candy did that, and with the help of the bank, they watched activity on her credit cards and bank account over the next couple of weeks. Whoever picked the wallet up must have only wanted the cash because no checks were written, and no credit card charges were made.

The first of the month rolled around and the city's bank statements came in. Candy was on her computer balancing the bank statements when she noticed some transactions that shouldn't have been on this one particular bank statement. After closer examination of the account, Candy realized that some of her personal bills that she had posted on *bill pay* had come out of the city account. The blood drained from Candy's face. She immediately started trying to figure out how that could have happened. Apparently when she closed her bank account and opened a new one, the bank had somehow started taking her personal transactions out of the city account. Candy was the primary signature on all of the city accounts. The bank clerk must have seen Candy's name on the city account, assumed it was her personal account, and set it up for Candy's personal drafts to come out of.

Candy called Pat and told him what she had found. "I'm about to have a heart attack Pat. It looks like I've used city money to pay my bills." Pat could hear the panic in Candy's voice. He calmly said, "Call all of the council members and tell them what happened. Then get over to the bank and straighten it out."

Candy was able to get hold of three of the council members. Larry was away at a conference and he didn't answer, and Mark was working. She told the three that she reached what had happened. She told them that she was on her way to the bank.

Candy thought Tom acted a little strange when she told him about what had happened. He said, "I just don't see how that could have happened Candy."

"I don't either, but it did." Candy replied.

Candy went to the bank and spoke with one of the bank associates. The associate told Candy that she didn't see how

After All is Said and Done....More is Said Than Done

that could have happened. The associate asked Candy to log on to her computer, and to put in Candy's bank information. That way they could look at Candy's account to see what was going on. Candy then went around the desk and got on the associates computer. Candy logged into her personal account and posted a bill to be paid. After the bill was posted they looked at the transaction and it was drafted out of the city account. The associate was so shocked. She said, "Oh my goodness. I've never seen anything like this before. I better call the main branch." She got on the phone and made the call. Candy could hear her explaining what had happened. Candy spoke up. "I need a letter from the bank explaining that I didn't use city money to pay my bills on purpose." The associate said, "I don't know if we can do that." Candy said, "You can, and you will." The associate went on talking on the phone and told the other person what Candy had said. After she hung up the phone she said, "The bank vice president is going to write you a letter. I'm so sorry this happened. I can understand how upset you must be." Candy told the associate to transfer the money out of her personal account, and into the city account to pay the city back. The associate told Candy she would be back in just a moment. When she returned, she had the letter from the bank vice president that said *"it was a banking error"*. The letter explained that it was of no fault of Candy's, and the issue had been resolved.

In the meantime, Sara was on the phone with Carter telling him that Candy had used city money to pay her bills. Carter couldn't wait to talk to the city council members. He knew he could convince them that Candy was a thief. He would have her on the chopping block by morning.

Candy took the letter back to city hall and made copies for all the council members. She put the copies in their mail boxes.

The next morning Council members Darrell Morris and Mark Jackson were in city hall when she returned from the post office. When she saw Mark she said, "Hey, I need to talk to you about something." He just waved her off and said, "I know, Darrell already told me. I saw those copies of that letter in the mail boxes. You need to get those letters out of there and shred them. Nobody needs to know about this."

Candy couldn't understand why he would tell her to do that. She took the letters out of the boxes, but she still had the original.

Darrell started asking Candy some questions. She really didn't think anything about it. "Do they talk to you about embezzlement at those conferences?" Candy just thought he wanted to talk shop with her. "Oh yea. You wouldn't believe some of the stuff people can come up with to steal money." She proceeded to tell him about some of the things that she had heard about. She had no idea that he suspected her of embezzlement.

Later that day Mark went into Candy's office and said, "I need to tell you something. The other council members don't want you to know this yet, but we think it would be a good idea to hire someone who would be City Clerk and City Manager. I know you tried it, and you said you wouldn't do it anymore, so we were thinking about hiring someone who would."

Candy felt like she had been slapped. "Let me understand this. You are asking me to resign so you can hire someone else for my job."

Mark was so hyper, Candy wasn't sure she understood what he really wanted. Mark started talking in spurts. It was hard for Candy to keep up. "You only have one year left before you could retire. We don't want you to leave right away. That's why the council didn't want you to know about this. They're

After All is Said and Done....More is Said Than Done

afraid you'll just walk out."

And that's exactly what was going through Candy's mind.

Mark continued. "I've already checked with the retirement company, and they said for you to take early retirement, the city could make a cash contribution to your retirement. They said about forty thousand dollars would be a fair amount. Would you be willing to do that? Now don't be upset. It has nothing to do with your work. You're the best. It's just time to make some changes. It's all about progress - just progress."

Candy was having a hard time holding back the tears. She said, "I'll think about it and let you know."

Mark said, "Okay, okay, just think about it. Now you know I'm just trying to be up front with you. The other council members didn't want you to know about it yet. They said they wanted to wait until next year, but I don't like the way they try to hide things from people. It's just not right."

That night Larry's family was having a birthday party for him. Candy had planned on going. She was so upset over what Mark had told her, but she didn't want to let Larry down. She just stayed in her office working until it was time to go over to the party in the community center. Candy had done a lot of thinking that day.

When Candy arrived at the party Larry rushed over to her. He gave Candy a big hug. "Hey babe. I'm so glad you're here".

Candy didn't want to bother Larry with this latest turn of events, but she did need to talk to him. "Wow there are a lot of people here. You're a pretty important guy. "Larry just grinned. Candy said, "Hey, I've got something I need to talk to you about tomorrow if you have time to come by city hall".

Larry winked at Candy and said, "Anything for you babe. "

About that time someone yelled at Larry to "get over there and cut the cake". Larry looked at Candy and rolled his eyes.

"Guess I better get over there"

Candy was still standing in the doorway. She wasn't planning on staying. She just wanted to make an appearance for Larry. Tom walked up beside her and said, "I need to talk to you. I found out what Mark did this afternoon, and I'm so mad at him."

Candy immediately had tears in her eyes. Tom said, "Mark has been calling my house, but I just can't talk to him right now. I'm just too mad. I need to talk to you later. Maybe I can come by the office in the morning and talk to you."

Candy couldn't say anything. She just nodded her head 'yes'. She didn't' want to cry. She turned and walked out the door.

Candy went back over to city hall. Before she went to Larry's party she had been working on payroll. She went into her office. She made a decision right then and there. She was not coming back. She figured up her time card and wrote her last pay check, then she left city hall.

After Candy got home she talked to Pat about all of it. Pat told her that she shouldn't decide what she was going to do until she talked to Tom.

The next morning Candy went in to work. Mark came by on his way to work. Candy told him that she had given his offer a lot of thought. "I have my vacation planned for October. That's six months away. You go ahead and hire someone now so I can start training them. After I take my vacation I won't be back."

Mark was so excited. "Really? You'll train someone for us. Oh this is great. It's just progress Candy. It's just all about progress. I'll tell the other council members. This is great."

Candy was thinking to herself, *You don't have to be so excited about it!*

After All is Said and Done....More is Said Than Done

Mark left city hall on cloud 9. He went to the police station and told Carter. Carter said, "I don't think you should let her stay till October. She'll mess everything up. That gives her too much time to really do some damage. We better do something to get rid of her now."

Mark started wringing his hands. "I hadn't thought of that man. Oh man. We better do something."

Carter said, "Calm down Mark. We'll think of something."

Less than an hour after Mark left Candy's office Tom showed up. "Candy, I am so mad at Mark. Is there any way we can repair the damage he's done."

"I don't know Tom."

"You know, the only thing that I haven't liked is that you take off on Wednesday, but every time I've asked you to do something, you've done it, so I don't know why that bothers me."

Candy told Tom that she had decided to leave in October.

Larry didn't call or come by to see Candy that day. Tom had talked to him about what was going on, so he decided to make himself scarce for a while.

Over the next week Tom started acting suspicious of Candy. Carter had put ideas into his head too. Candy knew someone had been going through her office at night when she wasn't there. Candy was very meticulous in her work, so if one paper was moved, she knew it. One morning when she came in someone had been on her computer and left it on. Candy didn't know who was going through her office at night, but there had to be a council member involved because they were the only ones who had keys to the office besides her and Sara.

Come to find out about it there was a whole group of people trying to catch Candy doing something she shouldn't. Carter,

Tom, Darrell, Sara and Adam had been searching her office looking for something incriminating. Problem was, there wasn't anything to find.

Candy had taken a vacation day off so that gave them more time to really look through all of the paperwork in Candy's office. Carter had them convinced that Candy was doing something illegal. He told them "That story she made up about the bank account being screwed up was a good one. She was planning on paying her bills with city money, then she was afraid she'd get caught, so she had to come up with something."

"Hey look at this" Adam shouted. He found where Candy had done a requisition for $250,000.00 from the Oklahoma Department of Commerce. The money was to pay contractors with a grant through ODoC. Tom called the bank to see if the money had been deposited into the city's checking account, and he was told that the money was not deposited.

"We got her!" Tom said. "She stole $250,000.00."

The truth of the matter was that once the requisitions were done, it took ten to fourteen days before the money was automatically deposit into the city's account, and Candy had just done that requisition two days ago. This little investigator group wasn't smart enough to figure that out though.

Tom said, "We better change the locks on the doors. We have to stop her." They all agreed, and Tom called the locksmith.

Candy was scheduled to attend a conference the next day. She had some papers that she needed to fax, but the office was closed. Pat was outside working in the yard. Candy called out to him, "I'll be back in just a minute. I need to go down to city hall and fax some stuff for tomorrows conference."

When Candy tried to unlock the back door of city hall her

key wouldn't work. She walked around to the front door, and that key wouldn't work either. Something was up. She got in her car and went back home.

When Candy got back to her house she told Pat that her keys wouldn't work at city hall. She said, "I'm fixin to find out what's going on." Pat listened as Candy made several calls to Sara. Sara wouldn't answer her phone. Candy left messages for Sara to return her calls. She never did. She also called Tom several times, but he wouldn't answer his phone either. On her third call to Darrell he answered. Candy said, "Why are the locks changed on city hall Darrell?"

Darrell wasn't a very good liar, but he was giving it his best. "We just think the locks need to be changed ever so often."

"Darrell there's something going on. What is it?"

"No, no, we just thought we should change the locks ever so often."

"You're lying to me. Why won't you just tell me if you have a problem with me? Does this have anything to do with the banking error?"

"No, no, it don't have anything to do with you."

By then Candy was so angry she was fighting to control her temper. "So how am I supposed to get into the office? Am I not allowed in there unless someone else is there?"

"Just for tomorrow."

"I was supposed to be at a conference tomorrow. Am I still supposed to go?"

"If that's what you were scheduled to do."

Candy could see that this was going nowhere, so she just said, "I'll talk to you later" and hung up.

The more she thought about it, the madder she got. She wasn't going to give up until she got some answers.

The town had a city attorney, Bob Thompson. Bob had

only worked for the town for a couple of months. The old city attorney, who had been with them for many years, had recently retired.

Bob was fresh out of law school. He knew absolutely nothing about municipal law, but he was ready to take on the world. He looked like a kid, and acted like a kid, but he and Candy got along well. Candy decided to call him.

Bob answered the phone on the first ring.

"Hey Bob. Whatcha doin?"

"I'm just sittin here watchin a movie. Whatcha up to?"

"I think I may have a problem. I'm hoping you can tell me what this is all about."

Candy proceeded to tell Bob about the locks being changed. Bob was floored.

"Oh man! They haven't told me anything. I have no idea what they're up to. Oh man." Bob said with a little panic in his voice, "Now Candy, don't go in there and quit."

"That's exactly what I'm gonna do."

"Don't do that. They can't run that place without you. It would just be a disaster. Please think about this. Don't do anything rash. This can be straightened out. I have an idea of what this is about. You have made some enemies on the city council, and their just trying to pay you back."

"I've made up my mind. I'm done."

***

The next morning Candy got dressed. Not in her usual work clothes. She put on tennis shoes, some baggy Hawaiian print capris, a t-shirt and ball cap. She got in Pat's pickup and headed for city hall.

When Candy pulled into her parking spot by the back door, the employees were all standing outside. Darrell and Tom pulled in at the same time as Candy. She waited for them to go over and unlock the door before she got out of the truck. As she approached to enter the door, Tom said, "Candy".

If looks could kill, Tom would be dead. Candy angrily said, "No, I have nothing to say to you. I wanted to talk to you last night. Now I don't! I'm just here to pick up my things."

Darrell was just standing there looking dumb. Darrell and Tom said at the same time, "Okay", and they stepped out of Candy's way.

After almost twenty years of working for the town, Candy had a ton of stuff at city hall. She went into her office and started packing. She had so many manuals and notes from conferences that she didn't want to haul home, so she shredded all the notes. There was lots and lots of stuff that she just threw away.

Candy noticed that Carter and another police officer had showed up. They were sitting by Sara's desk talking to her.

On one trip carrying boxes out to the truck, Candy saw Tom and Darrell sitting in the back office talking to one of the employees. They were taking them one by one back to the office and giving them instructions not to speak to Candy or the newspaper.

Candy continued clearing her things out. Tom walked into her office and said, "Do you need help with anything?"

Candy couldn't even look at him. She kept her eyes on what she was doing and said, "That desk out there that Mike uses is mine. If you could move it out back for me."

"Do you want them to load it?"

"No, just set it out back. I'll get it."

Tom instructed a couple of guys to carry it out. Candy would get Pat to help her with it later. She didn't want Tom doing anything for her right now.

The last box was loaded. Candy called Pat, and he came

and helped her with the desk. Candy asked Pat to take her keys, - that didn't work anymore, - her city cell phone, and credit card in to city hall and give them to someone.

Pat went in to city hall and laid Candy's things on the counter. "Here's Candy's keys and phone."

Sara was sitting at her desk and acted like she was afraid to get up. She was the only one in the front office. Pat just turned and walked back out.

"Are you going to be okay?" Pat asked Candy.

"Yep, I'll be just fine. You go on to work."

Candy spent the rest of the day unloading the things she wanted. Then she made a trip to the mission and gave them the rest. She had lamps, a Christmas tree, a coat tree... It looked like she lived at city hall.

Candy felt like she did when she left Charlie. Kind of empty and sad, but glad it was over. Well, she thought it was over.

After All is Said and Done....More is Said Than Done

Chapter 34

Word got out like wild fire that Candy had quit. It was the biggest story ever to hit Hereford. People immediately started making up their own versions.

The barber shop was one of the best places to get the scoop. Carter rushed right over to the barber shop so he could get the news out.

"You know the city council suspects Candy of embezzlement."

The barber shop was full, and all eyes were now on Carter.

One fella in a camo shirt, an orange cap, and chewing tobacco in his mouth said, "I don't believe that. I've known that girl her whole life, and I just don't believe it."

Carter shrugged and said, "That's just what I heard. Look at all that work she's been doing at her Mom and Dad's old place. She don't make that much money."

"She's probably in debt just like the rest of us!"

"Why'd she quit then? I think she knew she was caught. And did you hear about that grant money that never made it to the bank?"

"What grant money?"

Now Carter had their attention. He gave them his version of the missing grant money, and then he told them, "There's no telling how much she stole over the years."

Another man, dressed in kaki colored pants, a plaid shirt, and a cap that said "#1 Papa", decided it was time to speak up.

"I think if there is anything missing over there, they better look a little harder. I don't believe Candy did anything wrong, but I think she knows someone who did."

Carter wasn't sure who believed him, and who didn't, but he knew the story was out.

Chapter 35

The unemployment line was long but this was something that had to be done. Candy was scared, nervous, sad, confused, embarrassed ....

She waited her turn to file her claim.

When her name was called, "Candy Patterson - Candy Patterson", she looked around to see if she recognized anyone else waiting. This was the most humiliating thing Candy had ever done in her life.

Candy explained to the case worker why she quit her job. She didn't want to draw unemployment. She wanted to work.

The case worker was very nice to Candy. She showed her how to file her unemployment claims online, and how to search for work. Then she gave Candy a typing test, and did an evaluation of Candy's skills and experience. The case worker seemed impressed with all that Candy had to offer an employer.

Later that day Candy and Pat were on their way to Cale's house, when Candy's cell phone rang. It was her sister Natalee.

"Candy, I hate to tell you this, but there are rumors' going around that the city is filing charges against you. They are telling people that you stole a bunch of money, and all kinds of stuff."

Candy's heart sank.

"I knew they were up to something. I don't understand why they are doing this to me. If they had a problem with something, why didn't they just tell me so I could explain?"

"I don't know. I'm just sick about it. They said the city council is having a meeting tomorrow at 11 o'clock. Something about a signature stamp. You should probably talk to a lawyer."

"I filed for unemployment today. That was hard. I've never been out of work before. It made me feel just terrible standing in that line, and now this!"

"You know Carter is behind all of this. I just hate that guy."

Candy hung up the phone and started to cry. She told Pat what Natalee had said, then Candy dialed Larry's cell phone number.

"Hey Babe, what's up? You okay?"

"Don't start with me Larry. I heard that the city is filing charges against me. What is this all about?"

Larry got quiet for a couple of seconds. Then he said, "I don't know anything about it."

"I'm so sick of your lying. You do know what this is about! I heard something about a signature stamp. Is this because I used your signature stamp?"

"I don't know. All I know is they said something about signatures at the bank."

"If this has anything to do with me using that stamp of yours, you know you told me to use it!"

Larry was sounding very nervous.

"I told you to use it once."

"That's a lie and you know it!! Candy was yelling at Larry now. "I used that stamp on every check I wrote, and you know it. You were too lazy to ever come by the office and sign anything! Now I'm going to have to get a lawyer. I was hoping after everyone got what they wanted - me gone - that they would leave me alone. All of you sit there and listen to that NUT BALL Carter, and you don't even realize what he is doing to you.! You have never stood up for me. "

"I'm sorry Candy. I hate that it has come to this. I'll talk to you later."

"NO! You won't talk to me. We're done talking!" She knew she would never speak to Larry again.

By the time Candy was full into the conversation with Larry, she was at Cale's house. Pat and Cale were listening to the whole thing. Cale wasn't' saying anything, but it showed on his face. He was ready to go pay Larry a visit.

Pat said, "I'll call Jackson Snow. He's the best attorney in the area."

After All is Said and Done....More is Said Than Done

Chapter 36

The newspaper had the big story the next morning.

"LONG TIME CITY CLERK RESIGNS"

There was a quote from Darrell, but knowing the Hereford Journal they didn't get it right.

"No, the City Clerk was not pressured to resign. I have no further comments."

And a quote from the city attorney.

"We are in an unfortunate situation here, but we will get back on track ..."

Jackson Snow was a tall cowboy in his late 60's. He had gray hair and a tanned face. He wore a starched white shirt, wrangler jeans, and cowboy boots. He was known for winning at least one really big case, and everyone wanted him for their lawyer.

Pat and Candy walked into Jackson's office at 8 AM. Neither of them had slept all night. Candy cried most of the night. She just couldn't believe that people could be so cruel and mean.

Candy told Jackson about why she quit her job, and her conversation with Larry.

"Sounds to me like those people down there are just like the rest of these little hick town city council members." Jackson said. "You haven't done anything wrong. You need to keep your head up, and don't let them do this to you."

Pat was holding Candy's hand as Jackson spoke. Pat couldn't stand to see Candy so sad. He looked at Jackson and said, "They are having a special council meeting today. I think she should go to the meeting."

"Sure, yea, go. Matter of fact, go to that meeting and demand a state audit. Let's just sit on this for now and see what they do."

Chapter 37

When Candy and Pat got home Cale was there waiting for them, and Abby was on her way. Cale had called Abby and filled her in on what had happened.

Abby had grown into a beautiful confident woman. Candy knew even when Abby was a child that she would one day be beautiful and successful. Abby had long brown hair almost down to her waist. Her hair was highlighted with enough blond to really show off her features. She had dark brown eyes and long thick eyelashes. She was much taller than Candy. She could have been a model.

Abby and Cale were going with Candy and Pat to the city council meeting. Cale's wife Laura said she would be there too. She would meet them there.

People were already calling Candy and telling her they didn't believe "this trash". The people of Hereford knew Candy, and they knew she didn't do anything wrong. A few Hereford citizens told Candy that they would be at the meeting too.

Chapter 38

It was a day that Candy would never forget. It was a major turning point in her life.

When Candy's parade arrived at the council meeting, they all sat down in the back row of chairs.

Candy said, "Why are we sitting back here. Let's move up front where we can hear."

Abby said, "Yes, let's move. We want to hear what they have to say." Abby was ready to pounce. She wasn't going to sit by and let them do this to her Mother.

They all got up and moved to the front row. Larry was sitting at the head of the table in his usual spot. He looked like he hadn't slept in a week. He wouldn't make eye contact with Candy, or any of the others.

All of the other council members were there. The city attorney was there at the council table as well.

Some of the city employees had gathered at the back of the room.

A woman named Letha Pitts was there from the newspaper. She was a short, fat, and unkempt looking woman. She wore her glasses perched on the end of her nose, and kept a pencil stuck behind her ear. She was often seen with a cigarette in her mouth. Her hair had the appearance of pink cotton candy. She was always in a rush, and only listened to about half of what a person told her in an interview. She was known for never getting a story right. The quotes she put in the paper where never correct. Everyone just hated to talk to her because they knew they would be misquoted. Letha made the paper a lot of money though. People loved reading her misleading stories. Letha sat right on the front row beside Pat.

After All is Said and Done....More is Said Than Done

Tom looked at Candy and said, "Hi Candy, How are ya?"
"I'm fine." Then a little hesitation. "No I'm not. I don't know why I said that. I'm not fine."
Tom sheepishly said, "I know, I was just trying to be polite."
Abby shot him a look of hate. "Oh yea, now he wants to be polite!"
Pat whispered to Abby, "Hush".
There was one item on the agenda. It said,

1. *"Discussion and/or action on an internal investigation involving a former employee"*

Candy turned to Pat and said, "This meeting is illegal. The agenda item isn't specific enough."
Letha nodded in agreement.
The meeting began. Sara was sitting in Candy's usual chair. Candy looked directly at Sara, and Sara just shrugged her shoulders.
The roll was called. All members were present.
Tom made a motion to contact the State Auditor and request an audit. The motion was second by Darrell. They all voted in favor. Larry kept his head down as he voted "yes". Candy hated all of them right now.
A motion was made to adjourn the meeting. As soon as the meeting was over, Letha jumped up and started asking the council members questions. Then she looked at Candy. Candy said, "You know I can't talk to you, but if I could, I'd have a lot to say."
Letha smiled broadly. Her cigarette stained teeth was all Candy could focus on. "I know, but tell me anyway."
An elderly man named Lester walked over to Pat. He had been sitting on the back row during the meeting.

"Hi Pat, sure am sorry you guys are going through this. This city council is the worst I've ever seen. Is that woman who was sitting by Candy her lawyer?"

"No, that's our daughter. Thanks for coming. Candy really appreciates all the support she's getting right now."

"Sure, sure. Anything I can do let me know."

"I guess I better get Candy out of here. Letha has her cornered."

Pat stepped back over to where Candy was. He took Candy's arm and protectively led her out. He was already thinking about what Letha was going to put in the paper.

After All is Said and Done....More is Said Than Done

Chapter 39

The next morning the paper smeared Candy all over the front page. Letha did a bang up job of making Candy look, and sound, like a hardened criminal.

Candy wouldn't get out of bed. She was mentally, and physically sick. Every time she moved she felt like she would throw up. Cale, Abby, and Pat stayed with her. They checked on her constantly, trying to get her to eat and drink, but they weren't having much luck.

This went on for three days. Abby was really getting worried. She started trying to get Candy in to see a Doctor. Candy didn't have a regular family physician. She wasn't ever sick.

Abby called three doctors, and none of them could see Candy that day. One doctor's office recommended taking Candy to the minor emergency clinic. Abby talked to Pat about it, and they decided they had to get Candy some medical treatment. Now they had to convince Candy to go to the minor emergency clinic.

"Mom, will you please try to get up and get dressed. Pat and I are taking you to the doctor. You haven't eaten in three days"

Candy could hear the pain in Abby's voice. She hated what she was putting her family through.

"Okay. I'll get ready to go. "Candy   c o u l d hardly speak without crying. Candy didn't feel like going anywhere, but she just had to force herself to get up. She couldn't go on like this.

At the clinic, Abby asked Candy if she could go into the patient room with her. Candy was glad that Abby offered to go in with her. She never imagined that Abby would one day be taking care of her, instead of her taking care of Abby.

Doctor Fuller walked into the room. He was in his late 60's, maybe early 70's. Tall, slim, gray hair and glasses. Behind those glasses were kind gray eyes that sparkled. He had on his white doctor's jacket and black Rockport shoes with Velcro straps. He looked like you would expect any doctor of that age to look.

"How are you today Mrs. Patterson?"

Doctor Fuller's eyes were so caring, and you could hear the compassion in his voice.

Candy was drained. She had no color left in her face, and her eyes were so sad.

Candy started to tell the doctor how she was feeling. All she got out of her mouth was, "I don't feel so good". Then she broke down in tears. Abby's heart was breaking.

Abby looked at her Mother and said, "Mom, do you mind if I talk to the Doctor."

Through her tears, Candy said, "No".

Abby told Doctor Fuller that Candy hadn't eaten anything in three days. She told him a little about the mess Candy was in, and how humiliated and embarrassed Candy felt.

"It is just more than she can deal with. I haven't seen her like this since her Mother died."

Doctor Fuller was so kind. He checked Candy's blood pressure and heart rate. He talked to her softly the whole time.

"Mrs. Patterson, I'm so sorry for what you are going through right now. I'm going to give you something that will help you rest, and something that will calm your stomach. After you take this medication, try to eat something light. I think after a couple of days you will feel like eating again. Be sure to drink lots of fluids too. I want to see you back here in

After All is Said and Done....More is Said Than Done

a week, but if you aren't better in a couple of days call me."

Candy still had tears in her eyes. She nodded *yes*.

After they left the doctor's office, Pat stopped at the pharmacy and got Candy's medicine. When they got home Cale was there. He had some chicken noodle soup on the table for Candy to eat.

Candy was able to eat a little, and then she took the medicine that the doctor said was to help her rest, and went to bed.

The next day when Candy woke up, Abby and Cale had gone home. Pat was there. He just couldn't go to work and leave Candy alone.

Pat showed Candy the mail. She had received lots of cards from friends who wanted her to know how much they cared about her.

Candy felt better today, and she knew tomorrow would be better than today, and each day would help her heart to mend.

Chapter 40

Every time anyone told Candy they had heard some gossip about her, her heart sank. Candy was on an emotional roller coaster. One day a friend of Candy's called her to offer her support. "I didn't believe any of that crap when I heard it. People just love to gossip."

People thought that saying things like that to Candy would make her feel better. But it didn't. She appreciated the support, but just the thought of people talking about her made her heart sink. She wanted it to all go away. Candy desperately needed it to go away.

***

Laura asked Candy if she would keep Elizabeth every day. Laura's Mom was going to work full time, and her Grandmother just wasn't able to keep Elizabeth any more. Candy was glad to have Elizabeth with her every day. It would help keep her mind off of herself.

Then Laura broke the news to Cale.

"Cale, I'm not happy any more. I am moving out. I just don't want to be married to you anymore."

Cale knew that Laura didn't seem to like him much anymore. He tried to make her happy, but it just wasn't possible.

Now Elizabeth needed Candy, as much as Candy needed Elizabeth. They would take care of each other.

Candy was so thankful for Elizabeth. Candy never dreamed she could love a person as much as she did her own children, but Candy couldn't have loved Elizabeth any more if she had given her birth.

As the days went by, Candy and Elizabeth had a bond that could never be broken. They shared a life together. A feeling

After All is Said and Done....More is Said Than Done

for each other that only they could understand.

Each day after Laura dropped Elizabeth off at Candy's house, they had breakfast, and then Candy would put Elizabeth in the stroller and take her for a walk. Sometimes they stopped in the library, and picked up some books and videos. After they got back home, they watched the '*Mickey Mouse Club House*'. They sang all the songs with Mickey and Minnie, and they danced all the dances. They laughed and enjoyed every day together.

After the divorce was settled, Cale moved in with Pat and Candy. He said he wanted to be close to Elizabeth, and he knew he would get to spend more time with her if he moved in. He also knew that Candy needed him. Candy needed her family to be with her.

Candy and Pat liked having Cale there. They never got too much of having their kids with them.

A young woman that Cale and Candy had known for some time stopped by Candy's house one evening looking for her dog.

"I was just wondering if you've seen Midget running around here. That crazy dog takes off running every time he gets out of the yard."

She handed Cale a picture of a tiny little yorkie dog. Cale looked at the picture closely.

"Gosh, no I haven't seen him. When did you lose him?"

"I just got home from work, and he wasn't in the yard." With a motion of her hand, she pointed behind her and said, "I live just over two blocks."

Lynette Jennings was a cute young woman. She had shoulder length blond hair parted on the side. She had brown eyes, and a wide smile. She was dressed in scrubs that had her name printed on the right shoulder and '*Women's Clinic*' on the other.

Lynette had heard that Cale had moved in with his Mom and Dad. She was hoping he would be there. Cale had grown up to be quite handsome. His hair had gotten a little darker over the years. Now it was more of a light brown color. His eyes were still a light blue, which always caught people's attention. He was muscular and fit.

Cale turned to his Mom who was sitting on the couch.

"Hey Mom, I'm going to walk around with Lynette and help her find her dog."

"Okay. Hope you find him Lynette."

"Thank you Mrs. Patterson."

Cale and Lynette walked out the door. They were talking as they walked away.

Pat looked at Candy over his newspaper.

"Do you know that girl?"

"Yes, she's Walt Jennings's daughter. Seems to be a really sweet girl. Cale has always seemed to like her." Candy grinned at Pat and said, "I didn't think it would take him long to get on with his life."

"She's pretty cute, and she seems really friendly."

Three hours later Cale came home.

"Found the dog. He was back in the yard when we got to Lynette's house. That little dog could fit through the chain link. I told her that I'll come over and put some chicken wire around the bottom of the fence so he doesn't get out any more. She said she'd make sure she puts a leash on him when she takes him out until I get it fixed. I'll probably go over there after work tomorrow."

And so it was, Cale went to Lynette's the next day to fix the fence. Then he went back the next evening to watch a movie, and the next night to eat spaghetti, and the next night.......

After All is Said and Done....More is Said Than Done

Chapter 41

Abby decided that a vacation was needed. She had been planning a family vacation to Florida for months. She made plane reservations for Pat & Candy, herself, and Cale and Elizabeth. Then she booked rooms at the *'Disney Wilderness Lodge Resort'*.

Candy's fiftieth birthday was in October, and Abby wanted this trip to be a special family vacation to celebrate Candy's birthday. In Candy's heart, it was all for Elizabeth.

Abby had T-shirts made for all of them to wear to the airport that said "**OH NO! She's the BIG 50**".

Elizabeth was only two years old, but it seemed like she had been talking since she was born. She talked nonstop on their way to the airport. She was so excited. They were all pretty excited. She called Candy "Mama". The same thing Candy's kids called her Mother.

"Mama, I can't wait to see Mickey Mouse!"

"Oh me too. We're going to have so much fun!"

"Mama, is Hemo there too." That's what she called Nemo the fish.

"I think so."

"Mama, where does Mickey Mouse live?"

It went on and on.

They arrived in Orlando at 10:00 A.M. They got settled into their rooms. Cale and Abby shared a room, Pat and Candy shared a room, and Elizabeth was a floater.

They decided they would spend the first day just hanging out at the resort. The lodge was just beautiful. It had the feel of really being in the mountains in a lodge. Their rooms looked out over a swimming pool that was landscaped with boulder's and pine trees. Beyond the swimming pool was the lake where ferry's waited to take riders over to Disney World. There was even a make shift geyser that shot out water every thirty minutes. There were walking trails, and bike paths. The creators of Disney really knew how to do things up.

They had passes for all of the Disney amusement parks, and they had a whole week to forget about Hereford, Oklahoma.

There was so much for them to do, yet they had down time to relax. One day Cale and Abby went to one of the more grown up parks, while Candy and Pat stayed at the lodge with Elizabeth. Oklahoma University was playing football against Texas that day. It was being broadcast on ESPN, so while Pat stayed in the room watching the game, Candy took Elizabeth to the beach on the South side of the resort. They spent all afternoon on the beach, building sand castles, and looking for treasures. Then they laid in a hammock and took a nap.

Candy's mind drifted back to Hereford occasionally. She wished she never had to go back there.

After All is Said and Done....More is Said Than Done

Chapter 42

Candy had been filling out applications since the first week she quit her job with the Town of Hereford, but she wasn't having any luck finding a new job. She had been through dozens of interviews. Each time she left an interview she felt pretty good about it, then she would get the letter saying '*Thank you for applying but*'. She was beginning to get very frustrated. She really didn't want to quit keeping Elizabeth, but she just wasn't in a financial situation that would afford her to stay home. If she hadn't been drawing unemployment, she didn't know what she would have done.

After returning home from vacation, Candy started applying for every job that she felt like she was qualified to do. She was even applying for jobs that she would have to drive an hour one way to get to. She just had to find a job.

***

One evening Candy was in her sewing room working on a dress that she was making for Elizabeth. Cale walked in and sat in the empty chair beside her. Candy could tell immediately that Cale had something on his mind. She knew her child.

"Hey Mom, I need to talk to you about something."

Candy was in the middle of sewing some lace on the dress. She knew that whatever this was, it was hard for Cale. She didn't want to make this any harder for him than it already was. She casually continued to sew as she spoke.

"Okay, what is it? "

"Well, Me and Lynette are gonna get married. "

Candy looked up at Cale. She knew he had more to say.

"Lynette is pretty sure she's pregnant. "

Candy hadn't ever thought about how she would respond to

news like this, but she surprised herself, because she actually felt pretty excited.

"I knew that's what you were gonna say! Has she seen a doctor?"

"No. She took one of those in home tests, and it was positive. She's gonna go to the doctor tomorrow."

"Does her Mom and Dad know?"

"She's telling them tonight too. She's pretty upset. We've been talking about getting married next summer, that is before this happened. She just didn't want it to be like this. She's afraid that people will say I had to marry her. I told her not to worry about what people think. We know we're not getting married just because of the baby. We're just moving things up, that's all."

Candy was so happy for Cale. He had found a woman who truly loved him, and he loved her. You could see it in the way they treated each other.

Candy told Cale that everything would be fine.

"I believe that everything happens for a reason, and God knew that we needed this little baby. I truly believe that. Now -- what are you going to do if Lynette's Dad wants to kill you?"

Then they both laughed.

Later that night when Pat got home from work, Cale gave him the news. He was thrilled with the idea of another grandchild, and he thought the world of Lynette.

Cale called Lynette to tell her how things went, and she had gotten the same reaction from her Mom and Dad.

Candy asked Cale if she was supposed to keep the news about the baby quiet, or was she allowed to start calling everyone. Cale had hoped that Candy wouldn't be upset, but he wasn't expecting her and Pat to be so excited.

"No, no reason to keep it a secret Mom."

After All is Said and Done....More is Said Than Done

Candy could hardly wait to tell her sisters and brothers. She would call Natalee first!

After All is Said and Done....
More is Said Than Done

PART 3

After All is Said and Done....More is Said Than Done

Chapter 43

There are three stages of life. Youth, middle age, and you're lookin' good. Candy couldn't believe she had made it to the final stage of life. She was now fifty-one years old. How had that happened?

Over the years she had lost a lot of family members. Annie's husband died shortly after Candy's mother. Then the next spring they lost her sister Maggie's husband. There was only two of her Mom's siblings still living, and none of her Dad's.

Maggie called Candy late one afternoon in January. "Hey Candy, did you hear that Aunt Loretta passed away last night?" Aunt Loretta was one of Candy's Mom's sisters.

"Oh no. I hate to hear that. She's been sick for a really long time."

Aunt Loretta was an eccentric woman. When she was young she was a model and quite beautiful. She was always a little high society compared to the rest of the family. She was married once, and had a couple of boys, but they weren't very close. They had busy lives, just like their Mother did when she was young.

When Aunt Loretta got too old to care for herself, the boys put her in an assisted living home. While living there she was the life of the party. She wore her white gloves to dinner each night, and even though her makeup didn't do too much for her appearance, she always had it on.

During her modeling days she lived pretty fast and furious. Over the years the smoking and social drinking took its toll on her appearance, but still, you could tell that she was once very beautiful.

Maggie went on to tell Candy about the funeral arrangements. "They're having her funeral in Amarillo. Me and Seth were thinking about going. Do you want to go with us?"

"You know, I think I would like to go. I know this sounds awful, but we always have such a good time when we go to funerals." They both laughed. "It's a shame that's the only time we see some of our relatives. I'd really like to see Aunt Loretta's boys. I haven't seen them since high school."

"Oh Good then! I'll call Seth and tell him you're going. We can just meet at his house. He said he'd drive."

***

Candy, Maggie, and their brother Seth, really enjoyed seeing everyone again. There were cousins that Candy hadn't seen in years.

The funeral wasn't like anything they had ever seen before. Aunt Loretta was in her white fur coat and matching hat. She had on her most expensive jewelry. They found out later that Aunt Loretta had arranged everything before she passed away. That was Aunt Loretta.

The music was old Patsy Cline and Carl Perkins tunes. They played three songs that were toe tappers. During the music Candy and Maggie got so tickled they were having a really hard time controlling themselves. Seth was trying to ignore them so he didn't start laughing too.

After the funeral was over they stayed around and visited with everyone a little more, then they said their goodbyes, made promises to keep in touch, and headed back to Oklahoma.

They stopped just outside of Amarillo to get gas. Candy went into the store to get some snacks for them, when her phone rang.

After All is Said and Done....More is Said Than Done

"May I speak to Candy Patterson please?"
"This is Candy."
"Hi, this is Amber Thrift. I'm with Comcord Communications. I was wondering if you are still interested in the job you applied for, as a communications specialist."
"Yes!, I am."
Candy had applied for so many jobs that she couldn't even remember what the job description was. She would have to look back through her papers when she got home.
"Great. You will need to report to the main office in Tulsa on February 17 at 7:30 A.M. When you arrive, go to the security desk and tell them who you are. They will have your name on their list and they will tell you where to go from there. Do you have any questions?"
"No, I can't think of anything right now. If I have questions may I call you back?"
"Certainly. We'll see you then on the 17th."
Candy was so excited. She had been applying and interviewing for jobs for ten months. She ran back out to the car and told Maggie and Seth about the call. They were so happy for her. They decided to stop off at the *BigTexan* to eat and celebrate Candy's new job.

Chapter 44

For the next three weeks Candy waited and wondered what her new job would be like. She really had no idea what she would be doing, but she knew that it was a good job. Her entire family and many of her friends had been praying for her for months. They all knew that God's timing was perfect, and the right job for her would be there when God said so.

Comcord Communications was a large corporation with offices all over the country. The main corporate office was located in Tulsa in a three story building. The company was one of the largest cell phone companies in America.

February 17th finally arrived. Candy dressed in her best business suit, made sure her hair was done just right, and at 6:30 A.M. she was on her way to rejoin the work force.

She walked into the lobby of Comcord Communications. Immediately inside the front door was the security desk. The security guard greeted her with a smile.

"Good morning Mam. May I help you?"

"Hi, my name is Candy Patterson. I was told that you would be expecting me."

"Yes Mam."

The guard had her to sign in, and he gave her a temporary pass. He told her to walk straight ahead, and then turn right at the corner. The elevators were on the right after she turned the corner.

"Get on the elevator and go to the second floor. After you get off the elevator go down the hall to the left. You'll see a sign that says 'Human Resources'. Go into that office and ask for Amber."

"Thank you."

"You're welcome Mam. Have a nice day. And welcome to Comcord."

Candy followed the directions that the security guard gave her. The building was very nice and modern. Lots of marble, leather, and mahogany everywhere.

Candy was asked to wait in a large conference room. While she waited, other new employees filed in. There were forty new employees in all. They spoke to each other as they waited. They had all been hired to do the same thing. Just that nobody really knew what they would be doing. All they knew is that it had something to do with customer service.

Amber was a young woman around twenty-five years old. She had dark hair pulled back in a ponytail.

"Good morning everyone! I'm Amber. I'll be walking you through a few steps this morning. The next few days will be orientation. We will go over all of the employee benefits, policies and procedures, dress codes and everything else that you'll need to know while working here. I'm going to take you into the training room where you each have assigned desks. Each desk has a computer on it with your name taped to the back of the monitor. When we get in there, please find your desk, have a seat and get settled. Someone will be in shortly to get things started. So if you would, please follow me."

All forty of the new employees herded out the door behind Amber and followed her to the training room. It felt like the first day of school. Here they were, each dressed in their best outfits, nervous and excited at the same time. Everyone had their own reasons for being there, but Candy was so thankful for a fresh new start. Nobody knew her here. She could get to know people, and she wouldn't be judged by what the papers had said about her. She had already decided to be very careful, and not get too close to people. She just wanted to work and NEVER go through something like what happened at Hereford again.

Everyone had found their desks. Actually it wasn't a desk. There were long folding tables set up. Each table had three computers sitting on it, and a persons name printed in big bold letters on a white sheet of paper taped to the back of the monitor.

As they were getting seated people were already grumbling about the working conditions. Candy said nothing. She was so thankful to finally get a job.

After they were all seated, a man in his late 40's, with a shaved head and a serious look, stepped to the front of the room.

"Hello everyone, I'm Danny McCoy. I am your supervisor and trainer. You will be in training for the next twelve weeks. Manuals have been placed in your chairs. I know there isn't much room in here, but once we get through the training we will be moving to a new office. The office is being built as we speak, and is scheduled to be completed by the time we finish training. The next two days will be spent going through orientation, then be ready to hit the ground running. We have a lot of material to cover, and there will be tests over each section of your manual. At the end of the training there will be a test over the entire manual. You will be expected to pass the tests. If you don't pass the big test, you will be given a second chance. If you don't pass it the second time …. Well….. I hate to say it like this, but you probably won't be working here anymore."

Danny's speech went on, telling everyone where the cafeteria was, restrooms, when they would be given breaks……..

Everyone listened intently. Right after the part about the tests, they knew they better pay attention. Candy could hardly

After All is Said and Done....More is Said Than Done

wait for the first break so she could call Pat and let him know how the new job was going.

Chapter 45

The next twelve weeks seemed to fly by. Two people quit in the first week. In the sixth week, one was fired. And in the twelfth week only five passed the first test, and one of them was Candy. All but three passed the second test.

Sitting in close quarters for twelve weeks, there was no way Candy was going to be able to not make some friends. She started talking to some of the people just a little at a time. She didn't want them to figure out that she was the Candy Patterson who had worked at Hereford. Most of the time she ate lunch in her car by herself, but occasionally she had lunch with the others in the cafeteria. There were a couple of guys that she became friendly with, and there was a group of four women that she enjoyed talking to.

There was a guy who sat at the computer next to her. He was in his mid 50's. He appeared to be in pretty good physical condition. He was fair complected, light sandy colored hair, and kind of rugged looking. He wore cowboy boots and western shirts. His name was Lane, but Candy called him Rancher. He told her that he moved to Oklahoma from California. He bought a ranch. "Twenty acres", he said, "I have a couple of horses. I just love to ride out on the back side of the twenty and just look around. "

Rancher said he retired from the Army. He tried selling real estate in California for a while, but that just wasn't for him. He said closing a deal on a house was just crazy sometimes. "We'd have thirty people at a closing sometimes. Out there a whole family of Mexicans would go in together to buy a house. Sometimes there would be ten or fifteen people on the deed. We'd have to get every one of them to sign off on the property,

After All is Said and Done....More is Said Than Done

and then there would be ten or fifteen other people buying the property. Just crazy. It was way too much trouble selling property out there. When I decided to move to the country I found my place on the internet. I bought it site unseen."
"Oh really."
"Yep. Moved here where it's nice and quiet. I'm gonna work a couple of years, then just kick back on my ranch."

***

Finally moving day had arrived. They boxed up all of their things before they left work on Friday. They were told to report to the new building at 7:30 A.M. on Monday morning. They were each given a desk number for the new building.

The new building was very nice but much smaller than the main office. Each employee had their own private cubical to work out of. They were told that they could decorate, bring pictures, and anything they wanted to make their cubical home.

Home indeed. Once they got settled in, the overtime started. Candy found herself working ten hours a day, six days a week. Within six weeks she was moved up a notch on the pay scale. In another six weeks she was moved up again. When bonuses were given, she was one of the few chosen to get one. She was working hard, learning a lot, and doing her best to keep her job.

Rumors had started going around again about the allegations by the Town of Hereford. Every time Candy heard rumors she still got sick to her stomach. She had prayed and prayed that it would all go away, but it just kept resurfacing. She couldn't understand why God was allowing this to happen to her. She begged God to make it go away, but it was a long way from over.

Chapter 46

It was October. Candy had been in her new job for eight months. It was a fast passed, constantly changing environment. People were being moved around to different cubicles for no apparent reason. Some were let go because they weren't working fast enough. It was a crazy place. People were grumbling about how working at Comcord kept you constantly on edge. They wondered everyday if they would have a job. Sometimes even people who appeared to be doing a good job were let go with no explanation, then there would be new faces in their cubicles.

***

Candy was quite handy, and when she decided to do something, she'd do it. She decided that her bathroom needed ceramic tile, so on her way home from work she stopped at Lowe's and bought the tile, cement, grout, sealer, and tools to do the job. She was working on the floor when Lynette stepped to the bathroom door and said, "Who is the Hereford city clerk?"

Candy looked at Lynette with fear in her eyes. "Why do you ask?"

"They just had something on the news about the Hereford City Clerk."

"They have to be talking about me."

"I thought maybe they were talking about Sara."

"What did they say?"

"I didn't catch much of it. Something about embezzlement."

Candy immediately got on the internet and there it was.

After All is Said and Done....More is Said Than Done

State Audit gives allegations of embezzlement against former City Clerk Candice Patterson. DA to determine if charges will be filed.

She went on to find a copy of the state audit. It stated that:

1) she had used the Mayors signature stamp on her overtime checks, without his authorization.
2) She was paid unauthorized travel expenses and a plane ticket for her husband was paid out of city funds.
3) There were questions regarding documents that she had shredded.
4) She had paid her personal bills out of city funds.

She just couldn't believe that Larry could stand by and let them do this to her. How could he do this? He knew she used his signature stamp on every check that went out the door of Hereford city hall. And there were explanations for all of the other allegations too! What a bunch of lies!!!!!! Ohhhhh!!!

Chapter 47

Candy cried all night. She felt like her life was over. She had seen how easily Comcord fired people. How would she ever get another job with this publicity?

The next morning she called Danny and told him she was sick, and wouldn't be in to work. Danny didn't tell Candy that he already knew what the problem was. Letha had done it again. Candy had made front page news.

Not only did she make the Hereford paper, she made the Tulsa and Oklahoma City paper, and the six o'clock news.

Candy cried most of the day.

"Pat, why is this happening to me? I just don't understand".

"I don't understand it either Candy, but you have to have faith that God will get us through this. Don't give up."

Give up is exactly what Candy wanted to do. She had always heard that God wouldn't put more on you than you could handle. Well, what about all those people who commit suicide. Wasn't whatever made them take their lives more than they could handle?

How was she going to face the people at work? What would she do if she lost her job? How, oh how, was she going to get through this?

After All is Said and Done....More is Said Than Done

Chapter 48

Candy knew what she had to do. The next morning she went to work early. As soon as Danny arrived, she went to his office.
"Guess you saw the paper?"
Danny snickered like it was no big deal. "Yea, I saw it."
"I know I look just awful today." Her eyes were so swollen and red. She really did look terrible.
"I want to explain to you what happened. I didn't embezzle anything."
"You don't have to explain it to me."
"I want to. Danny, I used the Mayors signature stamp on all the checks. Every single check that went out. I didn't just use it on my checks. Whether it was for an invoice or payroll. I worked for every hour I was paid. Actually I worked a lot of hours I didn't get paid for. The Mayor knew I used that stamp. He was too lazy to take time to sign anything. I've called him and told him I needed an original document signed, and he'd say, 'Just use my stamp'. When I'd tell him it had to be an original signature, he told me to just sign his name. I know I'm probably going to lose my job over this, but I didn't do what they are saying I did."
"I don't think you'll lose your job. You haven't been found guilty of anything. I'll talk to my boss about it, then I'll let you know what he says. Don't worry, it will be okay. I'm sure the real story will come out. I really am sorry for you Candy."
Candy went back to her desk and got to work. Several people came by and told her that they hadn't known her all that long, but they knew it wasn't so. One guy told her that it was obviously 'politics'. He said "You can read it all over that

story in the paper". Several people told her that they figured she must know things about people that she's not telling, and they are trying to turn things around. There were others who said she should demand another story in the paper with the truth.

Some people wouldn't even look her way. People who spoke to her every morning now turned their heads when they saw her coming. She felt so sad and frustrated. Why are you automatically guilty when you are accused of something? There is no innocent until proven guilty.

After All is Said and Done....More is Said Than Done

Chapter 49

Candy met with Jackson Snow right after work. He told her that he would meet with the DA and find out what he was planning on doing. He was sure there would be charges filed.

Jackson said, "I'll need at least five thousand dollars to get through the preliminary hearing. Then we'll go from there."

Candy knew this was going to cost a lot of money. She had already given Jackson a retainer, and she knew she would have to pay him more if charges were actually filed. "I'll get the money to you tomorrow."

"Candy, I don't know what the DA is thinking. I use to think I understood him, but not anymore. I'm sure he'll go after you hard on this deal. I'm sorry. I know you didn't do anything wrong. Hopefully we can prove it. I'll call you after I talk to him. He's such an arrogant SOB. Who knows what he has in mind."

The DA had only been in his position for a year. He was a former attorney who was known for protecting the innocent and getting convictions of the guilty. He stepped into an office that was a mess. People were glad that someone with the background and knowledge of Oklahoma law finally ran against the former DA.

Barton E. Clark was in his early 60's. Tall, gray hair. A nice looking man with a mission to get as many notches on his belt as he could. He knew that winning cases made news. And news about winning cases secured his job. He didn't care how he did it. Just as long as it appeared that he was getting the bad guys. He would get Candy Patterson, and he would get as much publicity as possible out of this.

That night Candy told Pat that she was going to sell their

place at the lake. "I've been thinking about it, and that will be the quickest way to come up with five thousand dollars. There's a guy that has asked me two or three times if I'd sell it to him. I'll call all my brothers and sisters and ask them if they want it first."

Pat hated for Candy to do that, but he knew she was right. That was the best thing to do.

Candy called each one of her brothers and sisters. Her brother Seth said that if nobody else wanted it, that he would like to buy it.

Seth already had a place on the lake, and Candy knew that he didn't really need it. He was just doing it to help Candy. It broke his heart when Candy called him crying, and he was going to do whatever he could to help her. He said, "I'll bring the money to you tomorrow, or I'll bring it tonight if you need me to."

"No, tomorrow is fine, or even next week. I'll tell my Attorney that I'll get the money to him."

"Now, if you decided after this is all over that you want the place back you just let me know."

After Candy hung up, she cried. She was so thankful for the support of her family. She knew that she would never be able to tell them in words how much it meant to her.

***

The next day Jackson called Candy.

"DA says he's filing felony embezzlement against you. I'm sorry. He also says he's filing charges against Pat."

"What in the world for?"

"He says Pat knew you were stealing from the Town. He says if Pat will quit his job, he won't file on him."

"That's blackmail. You do know that Pat campaigned for the former DA? He can't do this."

"I'm sorry, but do you really want to put Pat through this? You and Pat talk about it and let me know what you want me to tell the DA."

What in the world! How could this be possible? And why wasn't Jackson screaming mad about it?

Pat and Candy talked about it. Candy didn't want Pat to go through the humiliation and embarrassment that she had been going through. It was decided, Pat would quit his job.

The next day Pat went to his supervisor and told him. His Supervisor looked him in the eyes and said, "No. I'm not accepting your resignation. You are too valuable of an employee."

Later that day Pat was called into the office. His supervisor said, "I talked to the DA. I told him that he's not going to tell me who I can, or can't, have working for me. He might think he can push everyone else, but he's not going to tell me how to run my office."

Chapter 50

"What do I need to do? Maybe I should just go over and talk to the DA and explain everything to him."

You would have thought Candy had just told Jackson that she was leaving the country.

"No! DO NOT talk to the DA. Don't talk to ANYONE. I don't want you discussing this with anyone! I know you think it would be better to tell everyone your side of things, but don't do it. Hopefully the DA will let me turn you in, but I don't know really what he will do, but what ever happens, DON'T TALK TO ANYONE! "

Candy was almost in tears again. Her nerves were shot. "Okay." was all she could say.

Then in a little calmer tone Jackson said, "After the charge is officially made you will have to go before a Judge. The judge will set a bond then you will be taken over to the jail. After you post your bond you can leave until we go to court."

She was so afraid that the DA would send someone to her job to arrest her. When she went home from work she was afraid he would send someone to her house to arrest her. She spent the next forty-eight hours watching over her shoulder, and jumping every time she heard a car drive by. Then Jackson called her with the news.

Candy was at her desk working when Jackson called. It was 8:00 A.M.

"Candy, he's filing the charges today. He says he'll let the thing with Pat go. He did have the decency to call me so I could take you over to the court house instead of law enforcement picking you up. Can you come over to my office at 9:30?"

"Sure, I'll be there."

After All is Said and Done....More is Said Than Done

Candy went straight to Danny's office and told him what was going on. Then she called Pat - crying.

"I have a headache so bad. I'm going to go home and lay down for a little while."

"It will be okay. Don't let your faith waiver. I'll meet you at Jackson's office." Pat didn't know what else to say.

At 9:30 A.M. Candy and Pat walked into Jackson's office. Pat was so agitated. He couldn't believe it had come to this. "What do you think they will set her bond at?"

"The DA says he's going to ask for $10,000.00, but that's ridiculous. I think it will be around $1,000.00"

Pat asked Jackson if he had any recommendations for a bondsman. Jackson told him to contact Max Jones. He said Max had always been helpful when he needed him. He told Pat and Candy that he would meet them at the courthouse later. "The hearing will be at 11 o'clock. Be over there around 10:30."

After their brief meeting with Jackson, Candy and Pat went to Max's office. His office was an old musty smelling building on Main Street. The building was divided into four offices. When they walked in the front door they could hear classical music playing. It was coming from the office farthest to the back. They followed the sound of the music to the office that Max was sitting in. When he saw them, he reached to a Bose stereo system and turned the music down. Then he jumped up from his chair to greet them. "Come on in you guys. It's just me here today. Business hasn't been too good lately. "

Candy said, "I guess that's good for some, but bad for you huh? "

Max kind of snickered and said, "Yea, that's right. "

Max was a kind man. He felt just terrible for Candy. He told her that he had had a lot of innocent people sitting across from him. He told her that he would have her bond ready at the jail when she got there, and that she would not have to go into a jail cell. He said he would get her out of there as quickly as he could.

After they left Max's office, they went to Pat's office to wait. Candy was in a state of - - well, actually she felt nothing. She was just doing as she was instructed. Going through the motions and not understanding any of it.

It was time for court. An officer walked over to Candy and quietly said, "It's time to go". Candy had no idea she was going to be escorted by an officer. Pat sadly looked at her and said, "I'll be up there in the court room."

She got up from her chair and followed the officer. The officer spoke kindly to her. "Candy, we're going in the back way. I'm going to try to keep you away from cameras. The media may be up there, but I'll do my best to protect you."

There were three other criminal's walking to the elevator beside Candy. They had on orange jump suits, and were chained at the wrists and ankles. If Candy had been in her right mind she probably would have been humiliate, but right now, she felt nothing.

The officer escorted them to the front of the courtroom. There was a bench along the wall to the left of the Judge's desk. Quietly the officer spoke to Candy. "Candy, you can sit over here in the chair that I usually sit in. You don't have to sit over there with them."

Candy said, "Thank you."

Lots of people were coming into the courtroom and finding places to sit. Candy could see Pat standing by the back door. About that time Jackson walked in. He walked straight up to Candy. He had a look of authority.

"You don't have to sit up here. Go on back there with Pat."

Candy got up from the chair and walked to the back of the courtroom where Pat was standing.

Pat said, "What did he say to you?"

"He said for me to wait here with you."

The Judge entered the courtroom and the bailiff called "All rise". The Judge took his place. It was show time. "Mr. Snow, do you have a client here today?"

"Yes sir." Jackson walked to the Judges desk and motioned for Candy to come forward. She walked through the swinging gate and up to the Judges desk. Her head still pounding with pain, she could feel all eyes on her.

"Judge, I represent Candy Patterson. We would like to enter a plea of not guilty."

"Fine. Mrs. Patterson, do you understand the charges against you?"

"Yes."

"Mr. Clark, do you have a recommendation for bond."

"Yes sir. The State recommends $10,000.00"

Jackson spoke up. "Your honor, Mrs. Patterson has never been in any trouble, she has lived here most of her life, and she is not a flight risk. $10,000.00 is unreasonable."

"Fine. Your comments have been considered. Bond is set at $10,000.00. You may go."

The DA was fighting to hold back a grin. Jackson said, "May I take her over to the jail instead of an officer taking her?"

"Sure." The Judge never took his eyes off the papers in front of him.

Jackson motioned for Candy to walk with him to the back of the courtroom. "Let's step outside." They walked out into the lobby. "That was BS! I can't believe the Judge went along with that. He set bond at $10,000.00 for why! You're not a flight risk. Obviously he don't think so. He let you walk right out of there with me. That was decided between him and the DA before we ever walked in there. Well, go on over to the jail, they have your papers already from Max. You won't be over there long."

"You're not going over there with me?"

"No, you won't need me."

Pat didn't think he should be the one taking Candy into the jail, so he asked Les, a friend who was a deputy, to take Candy over. He told them that he would come over in a few minutes.

Candy got into Les' car. He told her that he just knew everything would be okay. Les was a Christian, and he knew that Candy was too. They talked a little on the way. The jail was only three blocks away. When they got there, Les told Candy he was taking her through the back just in case the media was there.

They went down a long hall that Candy had been down many times with Pat. She had walked this hall bringing inmates in with Pat. They stopped at the booking desk. Les spoke quietly to the booking clerk, and then he turned back to Candy. "The Sheriff told them to stop whatever they were doing, and to get you out of here as quickly as possible."

"That's nice of him to do that." Candy was still in a daze. Everything seemed to be happening like she was watching it, but not really there. It was very strange.

The booking clerk came over to Candy and told her that she was going to search her. She patted Candy down to check for weapons and such. She told Candy to take off her shoes and jewelry. Candy handed her wedding ring to Les.

Les said, "I'm going to go check on something Candy. I'll be right back."

After All is Said and Done....More is Said Than Done

After Les walked away, the clerk told Candy she needed to go do something real quick. She opened a big heavy sliding door on the wall behind Candy. "Wait in here." She motioned for Candy to go in, and then shut the door.

There were three other women in the room. They had on orange jail issued jumpsuits. They looked like they had probably been residents of the jail for some time, or they were maybe regulars, because they seemed pretty comfortable in their environment. There was a round table and some benches. Candy took a seat on the bench closest to the door. There was a T.V. in the corner. The channel was on CNN. One of the women kept looking at Candy. Another woman, in a gruff tone, said, "What are you staring at her for?"

"I'm just wonderin what the hell she's doin in here."

About that time the door opened. It was Les. He took Candy by the arm and said, "Come with me."

As they were stepping back out into the hall, the woman said, "What's she doin in here? She don't look like she ought to be in here."

Les said, "You don't know how right you are."

After the door was closed, Les said, "I can't believe she put you in there. If one of those women had known you were an officers' wife, they would have beat the dog out of you. Wait here a second."

Les left Candy standing there, but he was only gone a few seconds. The booking clerk returned with him.

Candy was then taken to have her mug shot and finger prints. The clerk was nice enough to Candy, but to her, Candy was just another criminal.

When Candy was released, she went straight home to bed. She had taken all the Excedrin that she could, and her head still hurt. She knew this was going to be a long and painful experience.

Chapter 51

The next day, Candy went back to work. She went to her cubical as usual and got to work. She knew that she was going to have to work harder than anyone else there, to hang on to her job.

She had gotten to know the four women that she sometimes had lunch with. Julie sat in the cubical right behind her, Paula sat in the cubical in front of her, and Sherry and Alison sat across from her. She was thankful that God had brought these women into her life.

Candy talked to them about her days at Hereford. She told them the whole crazy story. She seemed to especially click with Sherry and Julie. Her friends thought she should fire Jackson and start over. That might have been good advice, except Candy didn't have the money to do that.

They were very supportive, and she was glad that she had confided in them. She could tell that they believed her, and that was important to her. They told her not to worry about what anyone thought. They said, "We know the truth. All your friends know the truth, and who cares about the others."

Candy did care though. The old saying 'Sticks and Stones…' wasn't true. Words really do hurt.

***

Candy had a headache for two weeks. She decided she would go see her doctor.

The nurse took her into the examining room and checked her heart rate and blood pressure.

"Let me check your pressure again. It seems high."

The nurse checked Candy's blood pressure three more times.

After All is Said and Done....More is Said Than Done

"Why don't you just lay down there for a minute? I'll be right back. I'm going to get another nurse to check your pressure."

The nurse came back just a couple of seconds later with another nurse. The second nurse checked Candy's blood pressure. She frowned, and then wrote something on Candy's chart. The second nurse said, "Let's get Dr. Cooper to check this." Candy could see that both of the nurses were concerned.

"How high is it?" Candy asked.

"We both got 210 over 180. I'm going to get Dr. Cooper. You just lay there on your left side."

Dr. Cooper came into the room. "I hear your causing trouble in here." He said with a smile.

"Well, you know me."

Dr. Cooper checked Candy's blood pressure. "Yep, that's what it is, 210 over 180." He gave the nurse instructions to give Candy some medication, and to check her pressure every fifteen minutes.

After about an hour, Candy's blood pressure had gone down but it wasn't as low as the Doctor had hoped.

"Candy, I'm going to let you go home. I was thinking about sending you over to the hospital, but your blood pressure is going down now. I'm going to keep you here another hour just to be sure it's safe to send you home." Then he swiped his hand across his forehead and said, "Whewwww, I think I just saved you from having a stroke. Do you have any family history of high blood pressure?"

"Yes. Both of my brothers, and all three of my sisters are on blood pressure medicine. I've had this headache for over two weeks. Now I know why."

"Well, looks like you're joining your brothers and sisters. I'm sorry to tell you, but you will probably be on blood pressure medicine for the rest of your life."

Candy was very thankful that she hadn't had a stroke, but still, sometimes she didn't care what happened to her. What could be worse than all the other stuff that had happened to her?

Chapter 52

Your case is hereby set for Preliminary Hearing on January 19, 2010 at 10:00 A.M. Please contact my office to confirm receipt of this notice. Signed: Sincerely, Jackson Snow

Candy had met with Jackson on several occasions now. She never knew what his attitude was going to be at their meetings.

One time he told her that they could end up going to Jury Trial, and she needed to be prepared for the worst. "Because at the end of the day, I'm going home, but you may not."

Then there was the time that he told her, "You aren't guilty of a crime. You made a mistake, but that's not a crime. If we have to, we'll go to jury trial, but I'm not letting them get by with this."

Then he told her, "We just don't have any proof. I've told you to come up with something as proof of innocence, but you haven't."

It was an emotional roller coaster to say the least. Every time Candy got a call from Jackson's secretary, saying he wanted to meet with her, she was a nervous wreck. Jackson intimidated her, and every time she met with him she felt like her life was in his hands, and often times, those hands were not holding her side of the rope. She felt like Jackson and the DA was playing a game, and she was the game piece. She felt like Jackson didn't really care if he won this case. Candy didn't have a lot of money, but she had already paid Jackson a substantial amount according to her finances. He told her that if the case went to trial, she would have to pay him another $15,000.00 to $20,000.00. Candy didn't have any money left to pay Jackson. She didn't tell him that, but he knew it, otherwise he would have been working harder for her. Everyone knew that if you had a lot of money you could get out of anything, but innocent people are sent to prison every day. That is, the ones who don't have money.

Candy said, "I've been trying to get copies of my time cards. Even if I have no proof that I was authorized to use the signature stamp, I worked every hour I was paid. They can't make me work for free. I've contacted one of the new council members and asked him for copies of my time cards, but I'm not having any luck with that."

Jackson was in a fighting mood today. He said, "I'll just subpoena the time cards then!"

Candy was thinking, *'why didn't you do that a year ago'.*

A week later, Candy called Jackson's office. She spoke to his secretary.

"I was wondering if Jackson got copies of my time cards."

"I don't know but I'll check with him."

Another week went by, and another.

Finally Jackson's secretary called Candy and asked her to come to the office.

Jackson motioned for Candy to look at some papers he had laying on his desk. "Look at these papers. Is this what you wanted me to get?"

Candy looked at the papers. "No. That isn't time cards." What he was showing her was a page from her file that showed her remaining benefits. Candy did this report on each employee every month. It showed how much leave time they had accumulated, how much they used that month, and how much they had left.

"You mean you punched in and out on a time clock?"

"Yes, I did." Candy said in a frustrated tone.

"Are they just jerking me around?"

"Yes, they are. They have my actual time cards. Before I

left, all the time cards were filed in a cabinet in my office. Each employee had a folder with their names on the folders. Their personal time cards were in those folders. They're in a gray filing cabinet marked number three, in the second drawer."

"Okay, I'll just send them another subpoena and a letter explaining what we want. I'll tell them that if they don't send those time cards I'll be forced to take legal action against the town."

Seemed like Jackson was on Candy's side today.

***

The Preliminary Hearing was waved. Jackson didn't feel like they needed to have one.

Candy appeared in Judge Mackey's Courtroom with Jackson on the 19th of January. They went before the Judge, Jackson told the Judge that Candy waved her right to a Preliminary, and they left.

Two weeks later, Jackson's secretary summoned Candy to his office again.

"Well, I got this letter from Hereford. It says there are no time cards."

"What! Oh my gosh! I can't believe they are doing this. Shouldn't someone be in trouble for that?"

"Well now, we don't want to go making people mad. We have a good idea what happened to the time cards, but we don't want to go there."

Candy was totally confused now. Just who was Jackson worried about making mad.

Once again Candy came up empty handed. No proof.

Chapter 53

Time was flying by. Candy was still working a lot of hours. She needed to do everything she could to hold onto this job, and the more hours she worked, the less time she had to worry.

It was now August. Candy received another notice in the mail. This time it said she had a disposition hearing on August 20th. She called Jackson to find out what was about to happen next.

"Oh it's no big deal. We'll just go before the Judge. It will only take about five minutes." Jackson said.

"Okay, so I don't need to take the day off?"

"No. Just come by my office at 8:30. We are supposed to be in court at 9:00."

Since she never knew if Jackson was going to be fighting for her, or telling her that she didn't have a chance, Candy was nervous, sick, jumpy, and any other bad feeling you could possibly have, until she walked back out of Jackson's office. So for the next week she didn't eat, she didn't sleep, and she felt sick.

Candy went to Jackson's office on August 20th at 8:15 A.M. She sat in the lobby waiting. Jackson's secretary said, "You can go in now. "

Candy walked into Jackson's office. He sat behind a large mahogany desk. He appeared to be very busy. He glanced up from the papers on his desk and said, "I just wanted to make sure you made it for court. Just meet me over at the courthouse at 8:45 on the second floor.

Jackson's office was just around the corner from the courthouse, so Candy left her car parked in front of Jackson's office and walked around to the courthouse. She needed those

After All is Said and Done....More is Said Than Done

few minutes to think.

She found a bench outside of the courtroom and sat down to wait for Jackson. She waited, and waited, and waited, and waited.

It was 9:30. Candy was getting nervous. Where was Jackson? What should she do?

Pat had told Candy that he would be there as soon as he could get back from taking a guy to jail. When Candy saw Pat walking towards her, she was so relieved to see him. "Pat! Wasn't court at 9:00? People have been coming and going out of there ever since I sat down."

"Yea, court started at 9:00. Where's Jackson?"

"I don't know. He told me that he would meet me here."

"Wait here. I'll go in there and see what's going on."

A couple of minutes later Pat came out of the courtroom. "Jackson is in there sitting at the lawyer's desk. He must have come in the back way."

"You're kidding! I've been out here waiting all this time."

"Let's go in. I'll go over and let Jackson know you're here."

Candy and Pat walked into the courtroom. It was full of people. Most of the benches were full. There were people leaning against the walls on three sides. Candy spotted a vacant seat beside a woman who looked like she had a drug problem. She was twitching pretty badly, and when Candy got a better look, she saw that the woman only had a couple of teeth. She had tattoos on both arms, and she needed a cigarette bad.

The Judge was calling names in alphabetical order. Thank goodness he hadn't gotten to the "P's" yet.

This was not the way Candy thought a District Court would be. Lawyers were walking around, finding their clients, carrying on conversations. People weren't even trying to be quiet. Pat walked over to Jackson, who was having a pleasant conversation with another attorney. They were both laughing.

"Jackson, Candy is sitting right over there."

Jackson got up and walked over to Candy. "You don't have to go up there when the Judge calls your name. I'll take care of things."

"Okay. Thank you."

The woman sitting by Candy was called next. Her attorney motioned for her to come forward. She twitched, and jerked, and made her face do some things that were not normal. She got up and went with her attorney to the Judge's bench. Before the Attorney could say anything, the Judge peaked over his reading glasses and said, "Ms. Nelson it appears that we have a warrant for you. Looks like you had a previous drug charge, and you didn't take care of your fines. I'm going to reset this case for another day, because right now you're going to jail on the warrant."

The Judge motioned for an officer to come over. The Attorney didn't say a word. He just shook his head.

She was handcuffed and taken from the courtroom. Everyone had gotten quiet. They wanted to hear what was going on. As soon as the woman was taken out, the noise resumed.

When Candy's name was called, Jackson jumped up. "That one is mine Your Honor. We are working on a plea agreement with the DA."

Candy stayed in her seat, hoping people wouldn't know they were talking about her.

The Judge peaked over his reading glasses. "When are you going to have an agreement? Tomorrow?"

"Probably by Monday."

"Okay then, I'm setting this case for trial."

Jackson wrote something on a yellow note pad, and then walked over to Candy. He put his hand on Candy's shoulder and said in a pleasant voice, "Come over to my office tomorrow at 1:00. The DA wants to do a plea agreement. We'll talk about everything then. Now you two go home and take it easy."

Candy went back to work and told Danny what had taken place. He spoke to Candy with concern in his voice. "Just let me know what he says tomorrow. If you need time off, or anything I can do for you, let me know. Hopefully this will be over soon. I know your past ready for it to be over."

"Yes I am" Candy replied.

Chapter 54

"The DA says he'll give you a deferred sentence, you have to pay for the State Audit which was more than $41,000.00, plus you have to pay back all the overtime you were paid, and you have to plead guilty." Jackson spoke to Candy like they were negotiating the price of a car.

"That's a lie. I'm not guilty."

Jackson sighed deeply, and in a frustrated tone said, "This is the best deal we're going to get. You cannot say that, or the Judge won't accept your plea. Then we have to start all over again. Do you understand what I'm telling you?"

Sheepishly Candy said, "Yes, I understand."

"Okay then. I want you to come in and talk to my associate, George Smith. Rebecca will set you up an appointment for tomorrow. We need to get this over with. It's already gone on too long."

Rebecca told Candy to come in the next day at 10:00 A.M. to meet with George. Candy had no idea why she was meeting with George, but she was still just doing whatever she was told to do.

The next day, Candy walked into George's office. He was not there to be Candy's friend. He was just there to take care of business.

"Okay, I'm going to go over a list of questions. I'll put your answers on the paper. This paper will be given to the Judge. He'll ask you if you answered these questions on your own free will, and you'll say 'yes'. Do you understand?"

"Yes"

After each question George told Candy what her answer would be. When he was finished he told Candy to sign the

After All is Said and Done....More is Said Than Done

paper. She did as she was told.

"When you go before the Judge you will have to tell him what you did. I have written a statement that you will say. I made it as short and simple as I could."

Candy read the statement. *'I embezzled over $19,000.00 while I was employed by the Town of Hereford.'*

Oh God, please don't make me have to say that. The words were in Candy's head, but nothing came out of her mouth, but tears came out of her eyes.

George said, "Candy, don't think any less of yourself for having to do this. You are a victim of small town government."

Through her tears, she nodded her head. Then she walked out the door.

Chapter 55

The final court appearance was scheduled for September 22. On September 20, Candy was at her desk trying to focus on her job. After her meeting with George, she told Danny about the plea agreement.

Later that day, Danny told her that his boss wanted to talk to her.

Candy and Danny walked into his bosses' office. Danny seemed to be very nervous. Danny's boss, Andy Bullard, said "Candy, tell me what's going on. "

Candy was already about to cry. "Do you want the long version? "

"Danny has been keeping me informed. Just tell me about the plea agreement. "

Candy explained the situation to Andy. Andy seemed a little uncomfortable. "Candy, we think that if you plead guilty you will lose your job. Why can't you plead 'no contest'? "

"They didn't give me that option. " By then Candy was in tears. "I'll call my attorney and ask him about that."

As soon as Candy left Andy's office, she called Jackson and told him.

Once again he sounded aggravated. "I don't think the DA will go for that, but I'll ask him."

Candy was thinking, *yeaJackson you do that while you and the DA are playing golf this afternoon.*

Candy went back to her desk and got her head back into her work.

Candy didn't hear anything back from Jackson until 8:30 A.M. on the 22nd. Court day. "Hey, the DA says he'll let you plead 'no contest' if you can get a letter from your supervisor saying you'll be fired if you plead 'guilty'."

"Ok, I'll go talk to my supervisor and call you back."

Candy went to Danny's office and told him what Jackson had said. Danny said he'd go speak to Andy. A few minutes later Candy was called to Andy's office. Andy didn't waste any time. He said, "We've checked with the company attorney and he says we can't give you a letter."

Candy had expected this. She said, "I understand. I didn't think you could."

Of course they wouldn't give her a letter. They needed to leave the door open to do whatever they wanted. They hadn't decided if they were going to fire her or not.

Candy called Jackson back and gave him the news. Jackson sounded aggravated. "Well try to do something before court today. I'll meet you at the courthouse at 1:00. Court is at 1:30."

Candy knew there wasn't anything she could do. She met Jackson in the courthouse lobby. This time he didn't sneak in the back door. "Did you get something from your boss?"

"No, they won't give me anything."

"The DA says if your supervisor will call him and tell him that you're going to lose your job, he'll let you plead 'no contest'. Get on the phone and see if someone over there will talk to him."

Candy pulled her cell phone out of her pocket and called Danny's number. No answer. Then she called her friend Julie. Julie didn't know where Danny was, but she'd try to find him.

Jackson barked, "It can't be that hard to get in touch with your employer."

Candy nervously said, "I'm trying."

Jackson said, "You stay out here and keep trying to get hold of someone. " Then he walked away. A few minutes later he returned. "I got this thing postponed for two days. You see what you can do before then. "

"Why is the DA doing this? "

"He thinks you're lying."

Later that evening Candy and Pat were talking. Candy said, "Why is the DA acting like this? I just don't understand. Why will he not believe me?"

"He thinks everyone is a liar. It's really not personal against you."

The next day Candy talked to Danny and told him about the chaos at the courthouse. Candy asked Danny, "Who will actually make the decision on whether I still have a job. Do you think I should go talk to Human Resources?"

"Yes, I do. Actually you probably should have talked to HR in the beginning."

When Candy got back to her desk, she called the HR office and set up an appointment for the next morning.

Chapter 56

September 23rd, 9:00 A.M. Candy walked into the HR officer where she hadn't been since her first day on the job. She had a meeting scheduled with the director of HR.

There were two people besides Candy in the meeting. A witness was needed.

Candy explained the entire situation. She was told by the director that pleading guilty was not a guarantee of losing her job. They seemed to be sympathetic, so Candy was feeling pretty good about the meeting. After all, she was a good employee. They wouldn't fire her. Would they?

***

September 24, 2010

Jackson had told Candy that he would meet her at the courthouse. As Candy and Pat were walking up the steps of the courthouse, they ran into Pat's friend, Les. He asked if they would mind if he went into the hearing with them. He said, "I know there's nothing I can do to help, but I'd like to be there for you."

Candy wasn't really nervous. She was just ready to get it over with.

Waiting for them in the lobby, was Jackson Snow. He was dressed in his best lawyer suit. He told Candy that he was sorry things had turned out like they had. "This is so unfair. Are you sure you want to do this?"

Candy couldn't believe he asked her that. This was all his idea. He told her she didn't have any other choice! She looked at him with surprise, and said, "I don't know what else to do."

Jackson said, "Me either, but it's a shame."

They walked into the courtroom. Jackson took his place at

the attorney's desk. Candy, Pat, and Les sat on a bench at the back of the courtroom. There was only one other case set for that day. It was a guy accused of molesting children that he gave art lessons to.

Candy, Pat and Les sat talking quietly before the Judge came in. They talked about nothing and anything, but not Candy's situation.

It was just about time to start, and in walked Letha. Candy's face turned beet red, and her heart almost jumped out of her chest. Candy said, in no more than a barely audible whisper, "Oh my God, I'm going to be sick."

Pat reached over and took her hand. "It'll be okay. I think she's here on the child molester."

"Well isn't it her lucky day then. I bet she just can't believe she stumbled onto getting to hear my case today." Candy thought she would hyperventilate, pass out, throw up, or maybe all of the above. Then the Judge walked in.

After All is Said and Done....More is Said Than Done

Chapter 57

Judge Leon Berry walked into the room. "All rise."

The Judge appeared very serious, as all judges do. He had gray hair and looked very large beneath his black robe. He may have been a little guy, but at the moment he seemed huge to Candy. Huge and intimidating, just like Jackson.

The Judge heard the case of the accused child molester first. His attorney was asking that his client be allowed to continue to give art lessons to children. That was his only source of income. The attorney promised to have a signed consent from the students' parents that stated they knew about the molestation charge, and the parents would be present during the lessons.

The Assistant DA put on a good show. She was a young spunky blond who was ready to fight. She ranted, and she raved, and she objected, and said what a horrible crime this was, and this just could not be allowed!

The Judge said that the request was not unreasonable. He would allow the accused molester to give art lessons as long as the parent was present. He said the man had not been found guilty yet.

The Assistant DA shook her head, frowned a lot, said thank you Judge, and left. Now it was my turn. Letha was ready with her notepad and pencil.

The Judge looked at Jackson and said, "Mr. Snow, is Candy Patterson your client?"

Jackson jumped up from his chair and motioned for Candy to come forward.

The DA was there. He wasn't going to let an Assistant take care of this. He needed this publicity.

Jackson, Candy, and the DA walked forward. They stood in front of the Judges bench. Candy on the left, Jackson in the middle, and the DA on the right.

The Judge read over the charges. Candy cringed. She would never get used to hearing what she had been accused of.

Then the Judge went through the questions that Candy had been rehearsed on. She answered all the questions just like she had been told to do by George.

The Judge looked very sympathetic at Candy. He didn't seem convinced that she had committed this crime. The DA seemed a little antsy. He was holding his breath, hoping Candy didn't pull something, like changing her plea.

But she didn't. She pled guilty. But even as she said "Yes sir" to the Judge, she wanted to scream, "Why won't the DA believe me!!!!!!! I DID NOT DO THIS!!!!"

The Judge read over the plea agreement that Candy had signed. He looked over his reading glasses and said, "Ms. Patterson, have you read the terms of this agreement?"

"Yes Sir."

The Judge let out a big sigh. "Well, okay then." Then he signed the agreement, and said, "You have a right to change your plea within ten days, otherwise you will be required to follow the rules of the agreement. Do you understand?"

"Yes Sir."

"Alright then Ms. Patterson, ... you may go."

During the hearing, Letha was having a hard time hearing. She leaned forward. She put her hand behind her ear. She even asked the lady beside her what was said.

As soon as it was over, Jackson said, "Let's step out here in the hall a minute."

Letha had already jumped up, and was chasing the DA out of the courtroom.

After All is Said and Done....More is Said Than Done

Candy looked at Jackson and said, "I want to wait until Letha gets out of here."

Jackson said, "Someone must have called her. She wouldn't have known you had court today. The only one that could have been - was the DA. He's such a jack***." He stopped before he finished the word. "Sorry". Then he looked at Candy and said, "You're a really tough lady Candy."

"People keep telling me that, but it's not true."

"If enough people tell you, then maybe you'll start to believe it. I know one thing, if I was in a foxhole I'd want you in there with me."

Candy had to smile at that. She was thinking - *I don't think I'd want to be in there with you Jackson. That's one fight I'd be fighting by myself.*

Chapter 58

Headlines the next day said, "Former City Clerk Guilty". Letha made Candy sound as bad as any murderer. She should have been doing prison time for such a heinous crime. The real kicker was, this time she told the readers where Candy worked. As soon as the HR director saw the paper, he knew what had to be done. Candy was an embarrassment to the company. They couldn't allow her to continue working for them. If only their name hadn't been in the paper.

The next morning Candy went into work as usual. She was on pins and needles, but the day went on as usual.

Two days after the hearing, Candy went to work. That morning she had to change clothes twice. The first time she had a stain on the front of her shirt, the second time, she spilled coffee on herself before she got out the door. Then, when she went through the toll both in her car, she threw her change and missed the basket, so she had to dig out more money before she could get through the booth. She should have known right then that today was not going to be good.

After she got to work, she got situated in her cubical and started to work. She had been there a couple of hours when she was called into the office. She leaned around her cubical and told Julie that she had been "called to the Principals Office again". Julie looked more nervous than Candy.

Candy was placed on administrative leave pending a decision on her employment, but Comcord already knew what they were going to do. This was the chicken way to do it. She was told that she would be notified by mail of their decision. Candy was thinking, 'Do you think I'm stupid or something.'

Then, two weeks later, the letter came.

You are hereby dismissed from your position with Comcord Communications..........

She asked God to help her to understand. She asked God to at least give her a hint as to why she had to go through this. She asked God, and asked God, and asked, but she just couldn't hear the answers. What would she do now?

Then......she knew what she had to do.

The first phone call was to the Internal Revenue Service. Candy knew the Town of Hereford, the DA, Jackson, or nobody else could make her work for free.

The second call was to the OSBI (Oklahoma State Bureau of Investigations). The Hereford Police Department was going to be surprised when they got a call that the Department was being investigated.

The third call went to the State of Oklahoma Attorney General. He was quite interested to hear about the DA trying to force Pat to resign, and the Hereford City Council violations of open meeting act, and a multitude of other state violations. He was also interested in Sara's record keeping, or non-record keeping is more like it.

Investigations were immediately started. The Town of Hereford would have been less surprised by the space shuttle landing at the park. The newspaper, TV and radio had lots to report for a very long time. All of the council members and employees were publicly humiliated. Carter was a huge story. He'd never be able to work in law enforcement again.

Candy moved on. She wasn't going to let the DA ruin her life. She just couldn't live in Hereford any more. She and Pat moved to Tulsa. They sold the house in Hereford to their son Cale. He was now married to Lynette. They had a baby girl that they named Helen, and Elizabeth was now five years old. They needed the roomy house for their growing family, and they all knew that Candy's Mom and Dad would be so happy that Cale was living there.

Candy may never understand why things turned out the way they did, but she hoped that someday God would reveal to her his purpose. Whatever came next, Candy knew that God was always with her. God had carried her through this, and he would be with her in whatever was in her future. That was one thing that she was sure of.

PSALMS 57:1-3
1. O God, Have pity, for I am trusting you! I will hide beneath the shadow of your wings until this storm is past. 2. I will cry to the God of heaven who does such wonders for me. 3. He will send down help from heaven to save me, because of his love and his faithfulness.

Candy had a lot of misgivings about the Justice System. There really wasn't any justice. It's just a game of - See Who Can Win. After seeing, and hearing what the court system is all about, Candy learned that - After all is said and done …. More is said than done.

Would you like to see your manuscript become a book?

If you are interested in becoming a PublishAmerica author, please submit your manuscript for possible publication to us at:

acquisitions@publishamerica.com

You may also mail in your manuscript to:

**PublishAmerica
PO Box 151
Frederick, MD 21705**

www.publishamerica.com

CPSIA information can be obtained at www.ICGtesting.com
Printed in the USA
LVOW060502261011

252065LV00001B/46/P